D0205644

“Journalists are busy ruining other people’s lives.”

The bitterness in Strachan’s voice was evident.

“That’s unfair!” Gisella protested.

“Is it?” He turned to stare down into the fire. “I’m afraid I know too well what lengths they’ll go to get an interesting story.”

She took a deep breath. “If you don’t want to be interviewed, then of course I’ll respect that. I just need to stay one night in your Candle Tower. You won’t even know I’m there.”

Strachan looked up at that, with a glint in his eyes Gisella found hard to interpret. “It would be rather difficult to ignore you.”

“No, it won’t. I’ll stay in bed.”

He smiled. “It’s very flattering, of course.”

“Flattering?”

His grin deepened wickedly, and his gaze seemed to rest on the curve of her mouth. “Surely you’re aware that the Candle Tower is my bedroom....”

Jessica Hart was born in Ghana, but grew up in an Oxfordshire village. Her father was a civil engineer working overseas, so by the time she left school, she'd been to East Africa, South Africa, Papua New Guinea and Oman—and had acquired incurably itchy feet. She's had a haphazard series of jobs, including production assistant at a theater, research assistant, waitress, English teacher, cook on an outback property—in England, Egypt, Kenya, Jakarta and Australia, respectively. She's also worked with Operation Raleigh, selecting Venturers for expeditions, which took her to Cameroon and Algeria. Jessica now lives in England, where her hobbies are limited to eating, drinking and traveling, preferably to places where she'll find good food or desert or tropical rain.

Books by Jessica Hart

HARLEQUIN ROMANCE

3213—THE TROUBLE WITH LOVE
3231—WOMAN AT WILLAGONG CREEK

Don't miss any of our special offers. Write to us at the following address for information on our newest releases.

Harlequin Reader Service
P.O. Box 1397, Buffalo, NY 14240
Canadian address: P.O. Box 603,
Fort Erie, Ont. L2A 5X3

THE BECKONING FLAME

Jessica Hart

Harlequin Books

TORONTO • NEW YORK • LONDON
AMSTERDAM • PARIS • SYDNEY • HAMBURG
STOCKHOLM • ATHENS • TOKYO • MILAN
MADRID • WARSAW • BUDAPEST • AUCKLAND

If you purchased this book without a cover you should be aware that this book is stolen property. It was reported as "unsold and destroyed" to the publisher, and neither the author nor the publisher has received any payment for this "stripped book."

ISBN 0-373-03302-8

THE BECKONING FLAME

Copyright © 1993 by Jessica Hart.

All rights reserved. Except for use in any review, the reproduction or utilization of this work in whole or in part in any form by any electronic, mechanical or other means, now known or hereafter invented, including xerography, photocopying and recording, or in any information storage or retrieval system, is forbidden without the written permission of the publisher, Harlequin Enterprises Limited, 225 Duncan Mill Road, Don Mills, Ontario, Canada M3B 3K9.

All characters in this book have no existence outside the imagination of the author and have no relation whatsoever to anyone bearing the same name or names. They are not even distantly inspired by any individual known or unknown to the author, and all incidents are pure invention.

This edition published by arrangement with Harlequin Enterprises B. V.

® and TM are trademarks of the publisher. Trademarks indicated with ® are registered in the United States Patent and Trademark Office, the Canadian Trade Marks Office and in other countries.

Printed in U.S.A.

CHAPTER ONE

THE wind whipped the pale gold hair about Gisella's face as she leant on the dilapidated farm gate and breathed in deeply, unable to believe how cold and clean the air was after London. It smelt of rain and damp grass, edged with the woodsmoke tang of autumn and fallen leaves.

Billowing rainclouds chased each other across a gun-metal-grey sky and, across the river, the hills rose steep and austere. The stark, wild beauty of the higher slopes softened as they dropped into the gentler farming land along the valley, where the green fields were divided by neat stone dikes and the occasional whitewashed farm nestled into the hillside.

She couldn't have asked for a more peaceful spot. No noise, no traffic, no frantic editors, no deadlines. Just a solid, weathered cottage and this tranquil view. After the pressure of the last few months, she wanted nothing more. One more article to write, and the rest of the winter was hers to start on that long-promised novel. In this isolated part of Scotland there were likely to be, as Meg had promised, few distractions.

If it hadn't been for that letter, all would have been perfect.

A tiny frown darkened the smokiness of Gisella's grey eyes as she remembered the note she had received from the laird of Kilnacroish only two days ago. Yvonne Edwards, features editor on *Focus*, was insistent that she do the story as quickly as possible, and had rung her only yesterday wanting to know when Gisella would be able to send in her copy.

'Rumour has it that *Week By Week* are also planning a series debunking old myths and superstitions. I don't suppose they've got a writer in your class, Gisella, but, with the circulation figures the way they are, we can't afford to give any ground, so we're going to run your articles earlier than planned. If you can just send us that last piece on Castle Kilnacroish...'

Gisella drummed her fingers on the top bar of the gate, the beauty of the view momentarily forgotten. She had suggested that they drop the Kilnacroish article if time was so short, but Yvonne was adamant.

'It's a good story, and it's different. The whole point is that we're not doing the same tired old superstitions. You can bet your bottom dollar that *Week By Week* will just trot out the Loch Ness monster, but your articles will be different, especially since you've managed to spend the night in all those haunted rooms... No, Gisella, I think we need a story like Kilnacroish to round the series off. But the editor's breathing down my neck, so can you do it soon?'

The trouble was that it might not be that easy to get into Castle Kilnacroish. Gisella had written a charming letter to the laird, but he had been profoundly unimpressed and his reply had been nothing short of rude!

Still, she hadn't become a successful journalist by giving up at the first sign of opposition. It was frustrating to be balked at this stage but, if she wanted to make the break into feature writing, somehow she would just *have* to get herself into Castle Kilnacroish.

Meg had said the castle was not far from the cottage. Gisella wrestled with the gate, which eventually swung open, and headed across the field towards the river. She might be able to see it from there. Stumbling a little on the uneven ground, she grimaced as her heels sank into the squelchy turf, and remembered how much her shoes had cost.

She had some boots in the car, but she had been too impatient to see the cottage and take stock of her surroundings to unpack. Gisella hesitated, then shrugged. It was hardly worth going back now. She would just see if she could get a glimpse of the famous castle.

Engrossed in picking her way through the muddy patches, Gisella became aware too late that she was not alone in the field. Some sixth sense made her glance over her shoulder and stop dead as she saw that her path to the gate was blocked by a whole herd of bullocks, who had ambled over from the far corner of the field, curious about the colourful intruder.

Gisella eyed them nervously. She wasn't exactly *frightened*, but they did look awfully big at such close quarters! As nonchalantly as possible, she began to back away, but the bullocks followed her, watching her with blank brown eyes. Gisella bit her lip and stopped. They stopped too, lowering their heads and shifting their legs.

Did that mean they were about to charge?

Never had she felt so much a city girl! Gisella took another cautious step backwards and felt one of her heels sink ominously into a patch of mud. Wriggling her foot surreptitiously, she tried to free her shoe. The movement caught the eye of the most curious of the bullocks and it lumbered forward, startling a shriek out of Gisella. Abandoning her shoe with her nerve, she turned and fled to the safety of the tree, where she stood, awkwardly balanced on one shoe, and glared at her adversaries.

'Go away!' she spat and glanced longingly at the gate.

The bullocks took no notice. They had stopped just out of arm's reach, pressing together in a semicircle around her. Gisella's heart was thumping and she scolded herself angrily, humiliated by her own nervousness. She had outfaced far more frightening things than these stupid animals in the course of her career as a hard-hitting journalist, she reminded herself. There was absolutely no need to stand here like this. All she had to do was push them out of the way. Easy.

The rough bark of the tree dug into her back and the wind tousled her blonde hair, blowing it into her eyes as she stared hopelessly back at the cattle. They were breathing steamily in the chill November air. Surely they would get bored soon?

Suddenly, there was a shout from the gate.

Gisella's head jerked round, and then she leant limply back against the tree with a shuddering sigh of relief.

A man was striding over the field towards her, his dark brows drawn together in a ferocious scowl. He whacked the beasts on the rump until they snorted and blundered off to a safe distance, and then turned on Gisella.

She gave him a dazzling smile. 'Oh, thank——' she began with fervent gratitude, but he interrupted her.

'What the hell do you think you're doing?'

Gisella's smile blinked off in surprise at his hostile tone and she looked at him blankly. 'Sorry?'

Her first impression was of a dark, aggressive strength that was overwhelming at close quarters, and Gisella felt oddly winded, as if she had suddenly run into one of the granite outcrops that littered the landscape. The impulse to throw herself round her saviour's neck with grateful thanks evaporated at his expression.

'I asked what you were doing in my field!' he rapped out, the soft Scottish intonation sharpened by impatience. He had a square, pugnacious jaw and, below the scowl, a pair of the most intensely dark blue eyes she had ever seen.

And the most unfriendly, Gisella amended to herself. Even if he hadn't claimed to own the field, she would have known that he was a farmer from his dour expression and the tweed cap on his dark head. His clothes were equally typical: weather-beaten waxed jacket, worn green corduroy trousers and gumboots liberally coated with mud.

He was inspecting her with hostile eyes, and suddenly she realised how foolish she must look, teetering on one foot in the middle of the muddy field. Gisella had never enjoyed feeling foolish.

'I'm not doing anything,' she said defensively.

'You're trespassing, for a start! You've no business traipsing over my land without so much as a by-your-leave, alarming my stock!'

Gisella bristled at his tone. 'I might describe your precious cattle as a lot of things, but they certainly weren't alarmed! The beastly things tried to charge me!'

'If they did—which I think highly unlikely—it's no less than you deserve! You left the gate wide open, either through pig-ignorance or sheer bloody thoughtlessness!'

He was clearly furious with her. Gisella glanced a little guiltily at the gate, but refused to be intimidated by a mere farmer.

'So? There's no harm done.' She shrugged as casually as she could, turning back to encounter such a blaze of anger in the farmer's eyes that she recoiled instinctively.

'This is valuable stock!' he shouted. 'Much too valuable to be risked by your kind of stupidity! I don't imagine you gave a thought to what would happen if the cattle got out on to the road?' He gestured angrily towards the narrow lane that ran past the cottage.

'It's hardly the M1 out there,' Gisella snapped, limping over to retrieve her lost shoe. The cattle, she noticed, had wisely retreated to a safe distance from the farmer, but were still eyeing her suspiciously. 'In fact, you can hardly even call it a road,' she went on dismissively. 'They're not likely to get mown down out there, are they?'

'You'd be surprised,' the man said grimly. 'There are people like you driving around the roads as if they own them, just as they walk around the fields! And even if they survive idiotic tourists, somebody still has to be dragged out into the cold and wet to go and round them all up and put them back in the field. Not that you would care about that, either!'

He watched contemptuously as Gisella pulled her shoe out of the mud and slipped it on her foot, grimacing at the slimy cold. Her hair was the softest of golds, and it swung over her face as she bent, a slim and incongruously smart figure in the muddy field.

'Well, I'm terribly sorry if I was the cause of such a potential tragedy!' she said with some sarcasm. Unaware of his scrutiny, she tested her weight on the shoe experimentally and then looked up at him, pushing the swath of blonde hair behind her ear with a defiant glance.

The farmer didn't appear to be mollified. 'What are you doing in here, anyway?' he demanded.

'Just taking a little stroll,' Gisella said. 'It's not against the law, is it?'

'A stroll?' he repeated, incredulous. 'In *that* outfit?'

A faint flush stained Gisella's cheeks. 'What's wrong with it?'

Dark blue eyes travelled over her derisively. Eager to take stock of her surroundings, she hadn't stopped to change out of the clothes she had worn up from London. Long legs were encased in sheer pink tights, a deep purple skirt just skimmed the top of her knees and her jumper was dramatically patterned in purple and fuchsia-pink. She looked vibrant and glamorous—and undeniably out of place.

'I'm sure it's all very well on the catwalks in Paris,' he said sardonically, 'but it looks ridiculous in a Scottish field!'

Gisella shook back her hair, grey eyes bright. 'I didn't realise that walking across a field would be so fraught with rules and regulations,' she said crossly. 'How to close a gate. How to dress correctly. How to avoid offending overbearing farmers! I'd no idea the country would be so complicated!'

'What you call "rules and regulations" we prefer to think of as simple courtesy,' he said in a biting voice. 'Although it's obviously rather a difficult concept for you to grasp!'

Gisella's eyes flashed, but she closed her mouth firmly over the sharp retort that sprang to her lips. She wasn't going to get into a demeaning argument with some farmer! Tossing her head, she turned and began to walk, with as much dignity as she could muster in squelchy, teetering shoes, towards the gate.

The farmer escorted her, grim-faced, while Gisella did her best to ignore him. It was hard, though, when you had six feet of solid hostility striding next to you, and her eyes kept stealing sideways glances at his forbidding profile. She judged him to be in his late thirties, perhaps a little younger. He was certainly striking to look at, although his features were too harsh to be handsome and his expression too severe. Only the cool, well-cut mouth, with its hint of hidden sensuality, gave an indication of a rather more attractive man underneath.

As if aware of her gaze, he glanced down at her, and Gisella looked quickly away. She stared straight ahead, until a kerfuffle among the cautiously pursuing bullocks made her gasp with alarm and clutch instinctively at his arm as she stumbled over a hummock of grass.

'For God's sake!' he said irritably, setting her back on her feet. His hands were strong through the soft wool of her top and her heart jolted alarmingly. 'They're harmless animals!'

'Then why are they stalking us?' Gisella snapped, more unnerved by his hard, impersonal touch than by the cattle, but determined not to show it. She was uncomfortably conscious of where his hands had touched her, and made an effort to pull herself together.

A gleam of exasperated amusement lit the dark blue eyes, and the corner of his mouth creased intriguingly. 'This is Scotland, not the Serengeti! They're just curious. They're an unsophisticated lot—not used to bright colours in their field.'

It wasn't quite a smile, but it was enough to transform his forbidding expression into something quite different and infinitely more disturbing. Gisella concentrated on walking and on not noticing.

'I'll dye all my clothes brown before I go out for another walk, shall I?' she said, but he refused to rise to her sarcasm.

'A pair of boots might be advisable, too.' He cast a meaningful look at her shoes. Once they had been pink and elegant, but now were so clogged with mud as to be unrecognisable.

'Really? I'd never have thought of that by myself!' Infuriated by his patronising tone, Gisella swept through the gate and into the safety of the lane, only to find herself brought up short by a hand of steel at her elbow.

'Just a minute.'

'What is it *now*?'

'What about the gate?' he asked softly.

Gisella glanced at the gate still standing open. 'What about it?'

'You haven't closed it.'

'You close it if it matters so much!' She tried to shake herself free of his grip, but he merely shook his head.

'You opened it. You close it.'

Gisella stared up into implacable blue eyes for a long moment, searching for some sign of the humour that she had glimpsed so briefly, but found only an unmistakable will.

'Oh, for heaven's sake!' she muttered at last, wrenching her arm away, stalking over to the gate and pulling it to with a bang.

'Don't forget to fasten it properly.'

'All right, all right, I'm doing it!' she snapped. 'There, are you satisfied now?'

'Thank you,' he replied with equal sarcasm. He glanced over at her car, which she had pulled off the road on to the verge just past the cottage. It was a low red sports car, ludicrously out of place next to what was obviously his vehicle, a much battered and much muddied blue Land Rover. 'If you're looking for the main road, you'll need to go to the end here, turn left, and then left again at the village and follow the signs.'

'Sweet of you,' Gisella said acidly, 'but I happen to be staying here.'

'Here?' The dark blue gaze flicked to the solid, whitewashed cottage and then incredulously back to the girl before him, who was standing straight and slim in the wind, holding her shining blonde hair away from her face with her hand and watching him with antagonistic eyes that were as grey as mist over the hills at dusk.

'You're *staying* here?' he repeated with a frown.

'Surprise!' Gisella bared her teeth at him, wondering what had caused the odd flicker in his eyes a moment ago.

'For how long?'

'If it's any of your business, a few months. Till spring, anyway.' She could see the cottage over his shoulder. It looked solid and welcoming and she was looking forward to her stay. 'My name's Gisella Pryde,' she added. If they were going to be neighbours, they might as well introduce themselves.

'Strachan McLeod,' he grunted in reply, but he didn't offer to shake hands. He was frowning, as if searching his memory. 'Pryde? I've seen that name somewhere...'

'You might have read one of my articles,' Gisella said, with a hint of smugness. 'I'm a journalist.'

If she had hoped to impress him, she had missed her mark. The dark brows drew together and he looked at her with undisguised contempt.

'I might have known someone as thoughtless and irresponsible as you would turn out to be a journalist!' he said with some bitterness.

Gisella raised her brows. 'That's rather a sweeping generalisation, isn't it? What have you got against journalists?'

A muscle worked in his jaw. 'They're parasites, feeding off other people's troubles, stirring things up and inventing facts to suit themselves. The truth has nothing to do with it. Oh, no, all that counts is a good story, and they'll hound you until they get it!'

'I think you're exaggerating somewhat,' Gisella said coolly, wondering which journalist had had the misfortune to cross this disagreeable man before. 'Most journalists are professionals. The public want to be kept informed of what's going on, and that's what we do. Yes, it does mean stepping on a few toes occasionally, but they usually belong to vested interests who are terrified people will find out what they're really like. In any case,' she went on, seeing that he was patently unimpressed, 'I can assure you that I'm not likely to have the slightest interest in *your* affairs. I hardly imagine anything newsworthy goes on here, anyway. "Gate left open by marauding tourist. Cow on road. Gumboot discovered in sheep dip." It's hardly shock, horror material, is it?'

He looked at her with dislike. 'So what are you doing here? It's not like a journalist not to want to snoop around.'

'I prefer to call it research,' Gisella said coldly. 'I'm writing a series of articles on local legends and superstitions, and how they must have originated. So unless you've got a resident monster, I won't be bothering you!'

His eyes had narrowed suddenly, but Gisella wasn't looking. As she spoke, there had been the sound of movement in the back of the Land Rover, and her last word died on her lips as the most enormous dog she had ever seen jumped out and ambled over towards Strachan McLeod.

Gisella swallowed. He was a big man, but the dog's head reached almost to his waist. It was grey and shaggy and immensely strong, and she watched it warily as it rubbed its head affectionately against the man's jacket.

'It looks like you do have a monster after all,' she tried to joke, but her voice sounded high even to her own ears as she edged away.

'This is Bran.' His face softened as he glanced down at the dog and laid a hand on his head. 'He's an Irish wolfhound. He's not nearly as fierce as he looks, but he's a one-man dog and he doesn't take kindly to strangers.'

'He needn't worry—I wouldn't dream of interfering with him! Gisella said quickly, still eyeing the massive animal with horrified disbelief.

The dog had been regarding her with an unwavering stare, but at that he suddenly padded over towards her. Gisella took a hasty step backwards and cast an alarmed look at Strachan.

'He won't hurt you,' he said scornfully, but he watched the dog with a curious expression as Bran pushed his wet black nose at Gisella's hand.

He might not attack her, but he was certainly capable of crushing her! Gisella wasn't a great animal-lover, and a dog that size made her distinctly nervous. She would have liked to have whipped her hand behind her back, but didn't want to risk antagonising him, so instead she stroked the wiry head gingerly and was utterly astonished when Bran responded with another nuzzle and wagged his tail.

Still, she was relieved when Strachan called 'Bran!' sharply and the dog went obediently, but with evident reluctance, back to his side.

'You seem to hold a peculiar fascination for my animals,' Strachan said with a suspicious frown, obviously not best pleased to see Gisella welcomed with such warmth by his dog. 'First the cattle and now Bran. He's never done that to a stranger before.' Bran's eyes were still fixed on Gisella, his tail waving gently.

'You don't appear to be very at home with animals,' Strachan went on, watching Gisella brush herself down fastidiously where the dog had rubbed against her. 'You're going to find life round here a little fraught, aren't you, surrounded by stalking cattle and monster dogs?'

Gisella lifted her chin at the irony in his voice. 'I expect I'll get used to them. Frankly, from what

I've seen so far, I expect the humans to be more of a problem!'

'Indeed,' he agreed, the dark blue eyes resting on her thoughtfully. 'They usually are.' He turned abruptly, whistling for the dog. 'In the back, Bran!' he ordered, getting into the Land Rover and banging the door closed.

'Goodbye, Mr McLeod,' said Gisella, sugar-sweet. 'Thank you for the warm welcome!'

Strachan leant out of the window as he put the vehicle into gear. 'Let me give you two pieces of advice if you want a welcome, Miss Pryde,' he said, meeting her grey gaze steadily. 'One, don't go poking that journalist's nose of yours into things that don't concern you, and two, make sure you leave all gates exactly as you found them!'

Before Gisella could think up a suitable retort he let out the clutch, and drove off up the narrow lane, leaving her staring after him in frustration until the Land Rover disappeared around a bend.

Thoroughly ruffled by the whole encounter, Gisella stalked back into the cottage and shut the door behind her with unnecessary force. What an unbearable man! There was no need to carry on like that just because she had forgotten to shut his wretched gate!

She kicked off her shoes crossly at the door and then peeled off her ruined tights with a shudder before padding barefoot into the sitting-room and throwing herself down in an armchair. The worst thing, she reflected, was being honest enough to know that she had behaved badly! She shouldn't have left the gate open, and she shouldn't have let

Strachan McLeod rile her like that. If there was one thing Gisella hated, it was looking ridiculous. The only thing she hated more was having it pointed out—particularly by a man like Strachan McLeod!

Like that of many quick-tempered people, Gisella's anger didn't last long. After scowling at the wood-burning stove for a few minutes, she gave a reluctant grin as her sense of humour began to reassert itself. She must have looked daft in her smart, city clothes, pinned one-legged against the tree by a load of cows! No wonder Strachan McLeod had looked contemptuous.

She should have been charming and apologetic, instead of snapping back at him like that. If she was to spend the winter here, there was no point in antagonising her neighbours. Gisella's eyes took on a smoky hue as she studied the deep pink varnish on her toenails and wondered whether Strachan McLeod would have been at all receptive to her charm. Probably not, she decided. He didn't look like a man who would be easily charmed.

Unconsciously, Gisella sighed. It might have been worth the effort to have seen him smile.

The next time she saw him, she would make an extra effort to be pleasant. Gisella's mind drifted in pleasurable anticipation of the scene. The hostility would drop from Strachan McLeod's blue eyes, and he would smile, surprised and delighted to discover what a charming person she had turned out to be. He might even apologise for having so misjudged her at their unfortunate first meeting . . .

But this was going a little far for even Gisella's vivid imagination. She would do without the apology, but she was determined to make him realise just how nice she could be when she tried!

In the meantime, she still had to write that article for Yvonne. Rather guiltily, Gisella realised that she had wasted enough time thinking about Strachan McLeod. Pushing him firmly from her mind, she shook herself back to practicality and her more immediate problem.

How was she going to get into Castle Kilnacroish?

CHAPTER TWO

IF ONLY she hadn't had to spend the last month working on the Wightman case! Normally Gisella would have spent some time on research before she approached the laird but when her old paper had asked her to do a follow-up on her big scoop last year she had felt unable to refuse. It had turned out to be a much bigger story than she had anticipated, which was why she was sitting here with absolutely no idea about the best way to tackle the unhelpful laird of Kilnacroish!

Gisella suppressed a sigh. She was very tired, and not just because of the long drive from London. The frantic pressure of the last few months had taken its toll, and she was longing to have some time to herself. If she could just get this story out of the way, she would be able to relax and begin work on that novel she had promised herself for so long.

But Castle Kilnacroish came first.

She would just have to get on with it. Gisella sat up and pushed all thoughts of tiredness aside. She could do some local research—and who better to start with than Meg? She ought to let her know she had arrived safely, anyway.

Her bare toes were cold, and Gisella curled her legs beneath her in the chair as she reached for the telephone.

Meg had been her closest friend at university, and although they had since gone their separate ways—Gisella to London and journalism, Meg to marriage to a Scottish solicitor—they had kept in touch, and Gisella had jumped at Meg's offer to find her a quiet cottage near by to rent for the winter.

It was Meg who had casually mentioned Castle Kilnacroish when Gisella had first told her about the series of articles she was writing about local superstitions, and she was eager to know if Gisella had made any progress.

'Have you heard back from the laird yet?' she asked, after they had exchanged the usual greetings.

'I most certainly have!' Gisella said, recalled to her sense of grievance. 'Listen to this, Meg.' She rifled through her bag for the letter and spread it out on her lap as she read it to her friend.

'"Dear Miss Pryde"—that's the nice bit!—"Castle Kilnacroish is not, and never has been, open to the public, and I am not inclined to make an exception in order to satisfy the vulgar and sensationalist demands of the media. Your request to not only visit, but spend a night in the Candle Tower, appears as nothing less than a gross invasion of my privacy, and I have no hesitation in refusing. In the circumstances, I must ask you to make no references to Castle Kilnacroish or any superstitions attached to it in your articles." He's just signed it "Kilnacroish"—sheer arrogance if you ask me!' Gisella refolded the letter crossly. 'Well, what do you think of that?'

'He certainly doesn't seem too keen on the idea,' Meg said cautiously.

'He's obviously completely misunderstood my letter,' grumbled Gisella. 'I *told* him I wanted to concentrate on the historical and psychological bases to different superstitions. I don't see what's sensationalist about that! Castle Kilnacroish fits perfectly into the pattern of the other articles I've done for this series: a reputedly haunted place which is still lived in today. Nobody else has objected to me staying to describe the atmosphere, or to being interviewed about what it's like to live with a ghost. I've stayed in all sorts of places around the country trying to establish the background, and nobody else has accused me of being vulgar.' The laird's accusation had rankled with Gisella, and she glowered down at the letter in her hand.

'Perhaps he's afraid you're going to tear him to shreds,' Meg suggested. 'Some of your articles can be a bit . . . scathing. He might have heard of you.'

'This is completely different,' Gisella said crossly. 'This is a feature, not an investigative piece.'

'Either way, he obviously doesn't like the idea! If he's refused to let you stay, I suppose you'll have to abandon the story?'

'I can't.' Gisella told her how insistent Yvonne was being. 'I really can't afford to alienate her if I want to carry on writing features, especially now that I'm a freelance.'

'I don't understand why you gave up your job on the *Daily Examiner*,' Meg said frankly. 'Most journalists would give their eye-teeth to work for a national newspaper, and it wasn't as if they wanted to let you go.'

'Oh, Meg, I was sick of doing investigative work. I used to get a real buzz out of uncovering a big story, but now I just find it all a bit depressing. I really want to see if I can write this novel I've been talking about for so long, and, if I can just keep going by writing the occasional magazine feature, this is my big chance.'

Gisella twisted the telephone cord round her finger. 'Besides, I owe Yvonne a favour. She didn't have to give me a chance on features. All my experience has been on the investigative side, after all, and if you're good at one thing it doesn't necessarily mean you're going to be good at the other. And *Focus* has got a lot of competition at the moment. I don't want to let her down. So,' she ended with a sigh, 'somehow I've got to talk the laird round. Tell me, what do you know about him?'

'Not much, really,' Meg admitted. 'I've never met him. I gather he's not very sociable, but people round here have a lot of respect for him. I get the impression that there was some kind of scandal attached to Kilnacroish, but it was a long time before we came here, and nobody seems to talk about it.'

'Oh?' Gisella tapped her pen against her notebook thoughtfully. 'Damn, I *wish* I'd had a chance to find out more about him before I wrote!'

'What are you going to do now?' Meg asked curiously.

'I think I'll go up to the castle and ask him in person. He can only say "no" again. The direct approach is usually the most effective.'

'Especially when you look the way you do?' Meg added slyly. 'I suppose you're going to turn on that famous Pryde charm?' She sighed in mock disgust. 'It's sickening the way you only have to smile at a man to get your own way! None of them seems to be proof against those big grey eyes of yours.'

'Hmm.' Gisella made a non-committal sound, remembering Strachan McLeod. He hadn't been exactly bowled over! She had wedged the receiver between ear and shoulder and balanced her notebook on her knee, and was doodling while she thought. She found herself drawing the line of his mouth and scrubbed it out crossly. 'The laird's not married, is he?' she asked, bringing her mind back to the conversation with an effort. It might be easier to approach a wife.

'No.' Meg dropped her voice confidentially. 'Somebody told me he was engaged to be married to the most beautiful girl, years ago, but she called the wedding off at the last moment.'

'Why?' asked Gisella, ever the journalist.

'I don't know. It's all rather mysterious.'

'Perhaps if I get a chance to interview him, I can find out!' Gisella closed her notebook firmly on a drawing that was beginning to look suspiciously like Strachan McLeod. 'I think I'll try bearding him in his den, anyway, and if that doesn't work we'll have to get round him some other way. I don't suppose you could get to know him socially? That would help.'

'As a matter of fact, Neil and I are going to a supper party next week. Ellen knows the laird and she said she'd invited him, so he might be there, but Neil's made me promise faithfully not to let you involve me in any of your embarrassing schemes! He's terrified you're going to compromise his reputation.'

'Neil's such a dry old stick sometimes! He couldn't be anything other than a solicitor, could he? I don't know what you see in him, Meg.'

'There's no accounting for taste,' Meg said cheerfully. She knew perfectly well that Gisella and her husband were fond of each other in a mutually distrustful way. 'You'll probably fall in love with someone just as unlikely.' When Gisella snorted in disbelief she went on, 'I bet I'm right. It won't be with one of those trendy guys you're always hanging around with in London. When you fall in love, it'll be with a crash—and it'll be with the last person you expect!'

For no reason, Strachan McLeod's dour face flashed into Gisella's mind. At this rate she would be taking Meg seriously, Gisella thought with some amusement.

'Sure,' she mocked. 'Perhaps I'll fall in love with the grumpy old laird, too!'

'You never know,' said Meg portentously, and rang off to Gisella's hoots of laughter.

Gisella was still smiling as she put down the phone. She had no intention of falling in love with anybody—likely or not!—at the moment. She was going to get this story out of the way, and then she was going to spend a quiet winter by herself, concentrating on her book. She needed it.

Always in favour of instant action, Gisella jumped up and went into the little bedroom. It wasn't yet dark, and if she was going to tackle the formidable laird she might as well do it straight away.

Throwing open her suitcase on the bed, she tossed her clothes out impatiently as she searched for something suitable to wear. Striking as it was, she couldn't imagine her pink outfit going down any better with the laird than with Strachan McLeod! From his letter, she imagined him as a curmudgeonly old bachelor, with undoubtedly conservative tastes, so she chose a soft fawn-coloured skirt which looked suitably demure, with a silk shirt and a loose, deceptively casual cashmere cardigan. Gisella admired her reflection in the mildewed mirror as she fastened pearl studs into her ears.

She looked discreetly elegant, she decided, and certainly not the kind of person who could ever be associated with anything in the slightest bit vulgar or sensationalist! Confident of her own persuasive powers, Gisella was sure that in this guise she would have no trouble convincing the laird to change his mind.

Would Strachan McLeod approve?

The thought floated across her mind and lingered annoyingly until Gisella turned away from her reflection impatiently.

But it was hard to banish his lurking image from her thoughts. Deep blue eyes, the hard, exciting line of his cheek, the strength in his hands; the memories kept intruding as she combed her hair into a soft fall of pale gold and leant closer to the mirror to apply a warm raspberry-pink lipstick. As she outlined her lips, the quietly disturbing curve of his mouth sprang into her mind with a twist of memory so sharp that Gisella nearly flinched.

Unbidden, Meg's words came back to her. 'You'll fall in love with someone just as unlikely.'

Almost angrily, she snapped the top back on the lipstick. She was *not* going to think about Strachan McLeod. Absolutely not.

Outside, the clouds had rolled blackly together, obscuring the hills, and a steady rain was falling. Gisella held her raincoat over her head as she ran for the sports car. She had stopped in Crieston on the way through to stock up with some essentials for the kitchen and the back of the car was still cluttered with carrier bags. She should have taken them out earlier, but as usual she had been too impatient to look around before she finished unpacking.

Well, she would just have to do it when she got back. She would get soaked if she started running backwards and forwards now. There was no point in wasting all the trouble she had taken over her appearance by turning up at the castle looking like a drowned rat!

Castle Kilnacroish was marked on the map Meg had sent her to find her way to the cottage. Gisella turned it round on the steering-wheel to orientate herself while the rain splattered against the windscreen. It didn't look far. If she just went up here and then turned left, she might see some kind of sign to the castle.

She drove slowly along the narrow lane, peering through the windscreen wipers in search of the turning Meg had marked. Either she had missed it, or Meg had no idea about distance! Just when she had decided to turn round and retrace the route, a dilapidated farm vehicle appeared and stopped obligingly when she wound down her window to flag it down.

'Castle Kilnacroish? Well, now,' the weather-beaten old man said slowly. 'You'll be wanting the main entrance?'

'The nearest entrance will do,' Gisella said, blinking the rain out of her eyes and trying not to sound impatient.

'There's a way through the farm just up here on the right, but it's a rough road.' He cast a disparaging eye over the sleek red sports car. 'You might be better driving round to the main entrance. It's just a few miles further on.'

Gisella, typically, chose the most immediate route.

The old man had not been exaggerating when he said it was a rough road, she reflected as the low-slung car lurched over the track. The rain had filled all the pot-holes, and most of the once grassy verges had been churned to mud. Gisella bit her lip as the car scraped over a rut and wished, not for the first time, that she weren't given to quite such instant decisions. If the track got any worse, she would have to turn round. The old man had said there was a farm up here.

She squinted through the windscreen, hoping that the farmer would not object to her turning round in his yard. Surely they couldn't all be as unfriendly as Strachan McLeod!

As if her thoughts had conjured him up out of thin air, a Land Rover came round a bend in the track with jolting speed and only just managed to screech to a halt in time. The track was very narrow and the two vehicles sat nose to nose. With a sinking heart, Gisella watched the solid figure leap out of the Land Rover and stride towards her.

It *would* have to be Strachan McLeod!

She wound down her window as he stooped to speak to her, feeling at a distinct disadvantage in her low car. His square face seemed very close and his features were oddly familiar. She could see the texture of his weather-tanned skin and the way the hair grew at his temples. His dark brows were pulled together in a scowl and the blue eyes were as unfriendly as ever. He had, she noticed irrelevantly, beautiful eyelashes, thick and black and spangled with raindrops.

'You'll have to go back.'

No greeting, no 'please', no apology for nearly hitting her, Gisella noted sourly, forgetting her dreamy decision to dazzle him with her charm. Her nerves, already jangled by the near collision, prickled at his nearness.

'Why can't *you* go back?' she demanded.

Strachan sucked in his breath and spoke between gritted teeth. 'Because, Miss Pryde, I would need to reverse about quarter of a mile up the track to find a passing place, whereas *you* are only a few yards from the road. Doesn't it sound a fair thing to you?'

'Oh, all right,' snapped Gisella, adding sarcastically, 'since you asked so nicely!'

He glared at her, and she hurriedly put the car into reverse, but she was so unnerved by his looming presence that she stalled. Biting her lip, she refused to look at Strachan while she started the car again and began to inch back down the track. Her back windscreen was filthy and the rain was still pouring down, obscuring her vision even further.

'Damn!' Too late she realised that she had driven off the track on to the verge. The wheels spun furiously, but to no avail: the car just ploughed deeper into the mud.

Gisella put her head between her hands. She was normally the most competent of drivers. Why did this have to happen now, in front of *him*?

She looked up to see Strachan McLeod bearing down on her again, an impatient look on his face. Steeling herself, she pulled on her raincoat and got out of the car to face him.

'What the hell are you doing now?'

'It's obvious, isn't it? I'm taking the picturesque route!'

He sighed in exasperation, and Gisella noted with some satisfaction that her car was at such an angle that he still couldn't get the Land Rover past. No doubt, if it had been remotely possible, he would have driven past and left her to push her car out alone.

'You shouldn't be driving on these tracks in a car like this,' he said, walking round to see how deeply the wheels were stuck, and aiming what Gisella considered to be a quite unnecessary kick at one of the tyres.

'I was told this was the best way to the castle,' Gisella said mendaciously, and he looked over the top of the car at her with eyes that had sharpened unnervingly. 'I wasn't aware that it was being used as a rally course!'

'What do you mean by that?'

'You came round that corner at the speed of light. If I hadn't been driving so slowly there might have been a nasty accident.'

'If you hadn't been here in a quite unsuitable vehicle, I wouldn't have to be wasting my time now,' Strachan retorted unpleasantly. 'As it is, we're going to have to get you out of the way before I can get anywhere.' He sighed again and took off his cap to run a hand through his hair. 'You steer, I'll push.'

Much as she would have liked to refuse his help, Gisella got back into the car and clung grimly to the steering-wheel while Strachan bent down to push at the back of the car. After a few seconds he straightened, and walked back round to the front.

Leaning down, he put his face through the window and said quietly, but with obvious restraint, 'It would help if you started the engine.'

'Oh, yes . . . yes, of course . . .' Gisella was flustered, and furious with herself for being so idiotic.

They resumed their positions, and there was a good deal of muttered abuse from Strachan as he pushed and heaved and the engine whined in protest. The car refused to budge.

Wiping the rain from his face, Strachan straightened again. 'I'll have to tow you out. Got a rope?'

'In the back somewhere.'

Gisella opened the back of the car, and immediately an avalanche of plastic bags tumbled out and spilled their contents into the mud. A jar of caviare, Gisella's favourite treat, landed at Strachan's feet, and he raised his eyes heavenwards as he bent to pick it up.

'Very handy,' he said, handing it back to her with obvious contempt. 'I see you've brought the essentials of life with you to the wilds of Scotland!'

Gisella grovelled around, desperately shoving things back into bags, hating him and convinced quite illogically that it was all his fault. So much for her determination to impress him!

Eventually the rope was found and attached to the Land Rover. Gisella heaved a sigh of relief as the car slid slowly out of the mud and back on to the track. Strachan untied the rope and followed her as she reversed the last few yards on to the road, as if he could intimidate the car backwards by sheer force of will-power.

Handing her back the rope, he said in a dour voice, 'I suggest you take a few lessons in reversing before you venture on to a track like this again.'

Gisella almost snatched the rope from his hand. 'If you kept your rotten track in better condition there wouldn't be a problem. I'm surprised the laird doesn't have something to say about it.'

'The laird's got more important things to worry about,' Strachan said, but Gisella missed the sudden gleam of amusement in his eyes as she carried the rope round to the back of the car. 'What do you want to see him about, anyway? I assume that's why you're heading for the castle?'

'It's none of your business,' Gisella said ungraciously, slamming the boot shut.

'Suit yourself. But I can tell you now he's not there.'

'I'd prefer to find that out for myself,' she said shortly. 'Is the castle far up here?'

'A couple of miles—but if you're going to insist on going, I would strongly advise you to drive round and use the proper entrance.'

'I can manage perfectly well without your advice, thank you,' Gisella snapped, having almost decided to do precisely that, but abruptly changing her mind.

'Well, you'd better not be stuck on that track when I come back,' Strachan warned. 'I'm not going through that performance again!' He strode back up the track to retrieve the Land Rover, and a few moments later drove out and along the lane without a second glance at Gisella.

Still fuming, Gisella waited until he had disappeared and then drove with determination back up the track. There were no oncoming vehicles to stop her this time, but it was an uncomfortable, jolting ride and by the time she reached the end the gleaming red bodywork was covered in mud. She passed a farmyard—presumably Strachan McLeod's—and then a little later drove down through trees to a collection of stables and outbuildings.

In this dismal weather she was unsurprised to see no one around. She drove cautiously through the yard, which led on to the rear sweep of the drive. Following it round to the front, she parked under a tree and sat for a moment, looking at Castle Kilnacroish.

It was a bleak but imposing castle with a hotch-potch of round towers and fairy-tale turrets that gave it a timeless air. There could have been few alterations since medieval times, Gisella thought. After the first impression of grandeur, she could see that the castle was in need of major repairs and what once must have been a beautiful garden sweeping down to the river had grown wild.

Beyond the tangled garden, the woods encircled the castle on three sides, protecting it from the cold winds which must sweep down from the hills behind. Gisella could just see the barren slopes rise above the treeline before they disappeared into the lowering clouds. Sheltered as it was between the hills and the wide river, the castle needed only a magic wand to restore it to its former glory.

Swinging long legs out of the car, Gisella shut the door behind her abstractedly as she looked up at the massive stone walls. Its design was too haphazard to be strictly beautiful, and yet she felt oddly drawn to it. The sense of history was very strong. Which of the narrow windows had held Lady Isobel's beckoning candle? What had she felt as she gazed out of her bleak tower? It wasn't hard to see why superstitions had grown up in the shadow of the ancient stonework. If she narrowed her eyes, she could almost catch a glimpse of figures along the battlements...

She could not have asked for a more evocative setting for the place, but there was no point in thinking about how she would write it yet. First she had to tackle the laird.

The gravel crunched beneath Gisella's feet as she walked across to the enormous oak door. She pulled vigorously at the old-fashioned bell to cover her momentary nervousness. Its jangling echoed eerily, conjuring up images of shuffling footsteps and wild-eyed servants, but instead the door was opened by a plump, jolly-looking woman in an apron.

The laird was out, she explained, but he wouldn't be long. Strachan McLeod had been right about that, anyway. When Gisella asked if she could wait, Mrs Robertson, as the housekeeper introduced herself, offered to show her into the library. 'It's warmer in there.' Chattering volubly, she led Gisella across a vast baronial hall with flagstones underfoot and high stone walls gloomily decorated with deer heads and enormous antlers and faded tapestries. A magnificently grand staircase led up to a gallery which stretched the length of the hall.

Everything looked vaguely neglected, and it was bitterly cold. Gisella looked about her curiously. A suit of armour stood to attention by the door and she lifted the visor to peer inside, before dropping it hastily and stepping back as she recollected where she was. Meg always said she was incurably nosy, and she didn't want to give the wrong impression at this stage.

The library was a cosy, book-lined room, comfortably if shabbily furnished. It had a reassuringly lived-in feel to it, and its warmth was a blessing after the penetrating cold of the hall. Gisella looked around with interest while Mrs

Robertson stirred the fire back to life with a poker and then disappeared, bustling in a few minutes later with a tea tray.

'I'm away home, now,' she said. 'But the laird shouldn't be long. Perhaps you'd tell him that I've left his supper in the oven, but he needs to be sure and heat it through properly.'

Gisella wasn't quite sure when she was going to introduce this domestic note into her conversation with the laird, but she promised she would pass the message on.

Left alone, she sipped her tea while she warmed herself in front of the fire for a while, then, still holding her cup and saucer, strolled over to inspect the bookshelves.

There seemed to be an extraordinarily varied selection of books. Blonde head tilted to one side to read the titles along the spines more easily, she moved along the long wall of shelves, wondering if there would be anything about the history of the castle that she could ask to borrow.

Her eye fell on a stained leather cover and she squinted at the faded gold lettering. Something Kilnacroish. This looked promising!

Gisella was just easing it out of the shelf with her free hand when an ominously familiar voice spoke behind her.

'Busy snooping already, I see!'

She spun round, slopping tea into the saucer.

Strachan McLeod stood in the doorway. Without his cap and shabby jacket he looked younger and tougher. He wore a thick blue jumper; Gisella's first thought was that it was almost exactly the same colour as his eyes. Her next was that he was wearing only socks, and that his feet must have been cold walking across the flagstones.

'What are *you* doing . . . ?' she began, and then stopped. Bran had pushed through the door behind him and was padding towards her, grey tail waving in recognition. He seemed quite at home.

Gisella looked from the dog back to Strachan with foreboding. 'You're not . . . ?' she managed, unable to finish her question as the awful truth dawned.

Strachan smiled grimly. 'I am.' He shut the door behind him and went over to the fire. Holding out one foot to the warmth, he looked over his shoulder at Gisella.

She was still standing by the bookshelves, cup and saucer in hand, the ash-gold of her hair and the pale elegance of her clothes in sharp contrast to the dark background of books. Turbulent emotions chased across her face: shock, embarrassment, chagrin with herself at her own stupidity and with him for so obviously enjoying her humiliation. Bran, who had been standing wagging his tail at an unresponsive Gisella, gave up at last and threw himself down on the hearthrug with a disconsolate sigh.

Gisella hardly noticed him. She was thrown off balance by Strachan McLeod's unexpected appearance, by the disquieting lurch of her heart as their eyes had met, hers appalled, his dourly amused.

'Why didn't you tell me you were the laird of Kilnacroish?' she asked at last, putting her cup carefully down on a shelf.

Strachan shrugged. 'Why should I? It's not my fault if you didn't do your research properly. I'd have thought the least you could do would be to find out my name.'

Gisella mentally cursed the Wightman story. If she hadn't been working on that, she would have had time to prepare herself properly for this visit. As it was, she had put herself into a ridiculously embarrassing situation—not that she had any intention of admitting that to Strachan McLeod! 'You let me think you were just a farmer,' she accused him, rapidly regaining her poise.

'I am "just a farmer", as you put it,' he said sardonically. 'As you can probably see from the state of the castle, I can't afford a manager, so I have to farm the estate myself. "The laird of Kilnacroish" is an antiquated title now. I use it as little as possible.'

'You used it in your letter to me,' Gisella pointed out.

'Perhaps I guessed that someone like you wouldn't take much notice if you thought I was just a dim-witted yokel.'

'I don't think farmers are dim-witted or yokels!'

'Really? I'd never have guessed from the way you behaved this afternoon. I thought it wouldn't do you any harm to make a fool of yourself.'

She flushed. 'So you did know who I was!'

'Not at first, but when you mentioned your articles I remembered where I'd seen your name. I must say, I wasn't expecting to see you. I thought I'd made my answer to your request plain enough?'

'Oh, yes, it was crystal-clear,' Gisella agreed with feeling.

'Then why are you here? Or can I guess?'

CHAPTER THREE

GISELLA bit her lip. Since she was here, she might as well have her say, but she would need to choose her words carefully. To give herself time to think, she carried her cup and saucer over to the tray. 'I felt that perhaps I hadn't made myself clear,' she said carefully. 'I think you may have misunderstood my letter.'

'I'm not stupid, Miss Pryde,' he said flatly. 'I can read a letter as well as anyone else, even if I am a farmer. You want to spend the night here.'

'Yes...in the tower haunted by the ghost of Lady Isobel.' Gisella tried to sound reasonable. Surely it wasn't all *that* much to ask?

Strachan had turned to face her, his arms folded across his broad chest. His expression was not encouraging. 'The tower isn't haunted,' he said dampeningly. 'There are no such things as ghosts.'

'I know that,' Gisella said, affronted that he could even think she would be likely to believe in them.

'Then why are you wasting your time—not to mention mine—writing about something that's patently untrue? Not that it seems to bother most journalists!' he added in a biting tone.

'Obviously I *didn't* explain myself properly.' Gisella was hanging on to her temper with difficulty, and spoke with exaggerated patience. 'I've been working on a series of articles about how superstitions develop. For each article I've visited a different place that is supposed to be haunted and yet is still lived in, to contrast past and present and try and explain the historical reality behind the stories that have grown up. It's interesting to look at the psychological background to some of these legends, too.'

'You may find it interesting,' said Strachan, unimpressed. 'I don't.'

Gisella set her teeth and ploughed on. 'I've planned that Castle Kilnacroish will be the highlight of the series. It's a particularly romantic story.'

'Romantic?' Strachan looked at her incredulously. 'I'd hardly call it that.'

'Of course it is,' she insisted. Wandering over to the window, she looked out at the rain while she remembered all she had read about Castle Kilnacroish. Outside, a grim, grey dusk was gathering, much as it must have done in the fourteenth century when Lady Isobel looked out at the same view. 'A gloomy Scottish castle, a beautiful woman left alone while her brutish husband is away fighting the English, a lover from a rival clan . . . how much more romantic can you get?'

'It wasn't very romantic when the husband came home and found them together.' Strachan's prosaic voice came from the fire and Gisella turned back to him. 'He tied Isobel and her lover together and threw them off the battlements. Not exactly a happy ending.'

'There's more to romance than happy endings,' said Gisella. 'I'm talking about a romantic atmosphere.' She rested her hands on the back of one of the shabby armchairs and leant forwards, eager to make Strachan understand. She could write a wonderful piece about the story and the atmosphere of the castle today, if she could only convince him! 'There must have been very strong feelings involved for a story to last over six hundred years. What is it about this place that makes local people still tell their children about Isobel and how she risked everything for love?' Straightening, she moved restlessly away from the chair. 'Why do they say you can sometimes hear screams on a dark night, as if someone were falling to their death?'

'The wind,' said Strachan. 'I should have thought that was obvious.' In contrast to Gisella's restless eagerness, he stood granite-solid before the fire.

His determinedly cynical attitude was beginning to make Gisella feel, perversely, as if she almost believed in the superstitions.

'I agree that the wind might easily sound like screams, but that doesn't explain all the superstitions, does it? What about the candle?'

'What about it?' Strachan said unhelpfully.

'According to all the accounts I've read, Lady Isobel's lover used to wait in the trees out there.' Gisella glanced out of the window, as if half expecting to see a ghostly figure lurking at the edge of the woods. 'When she was alone, she would light a candle and place it in the tower window. That was his signal to slip through the secret door and up a stairway to her room. They say that on dark nights you can still see a candle burning in the window, beckoning the lover on——' She broke off, realising that she was getting carried away with the story and sounding far from the sceptical journalist she claimed to be. 'Naturally, there will be some logical explanation for this effect.'

'Naturally,' Strachan agreed, but amusement lurked about his mouth.

'I'd really like to concentrate on the physical details,' Gisella said, trying to force her mind away from the unexpected curve of his mouth. If he gave in and smiled, he would be devastating! What would it take to make him smile, really smile?

His raised eyebrow made her realise that she had trailed off in mid-sentence, and she pulled herself together with an effort. 'Yes, the physical details,' she continued, with an attempt at briskness. 'How different is the room now? Does it have an "atmosphere"? Is there some trick of the light that might account for the mysterious candle flame? Is there, in fact, a secret stairway to the tower?' She stopped and looked at him hopefully, but he gave no sign of answering any of the questions. 'Those are the kind of things I'd be looking for, so you can see how important it is for me to stay in the room.'

'I can't see anything of the kind.' The momentary amusement had vanished. 'It sounds to me as if you just want to poke and pry about my home.'

'Of course I don't!' Gisella took a deep breath and counted to ten. 'I'd just like to explore that one room thoroughly. I wouldn't go near the other rooms if you didn't want me to. And, as I said in my letter, ideally I'd like to spend the night there. I've done that for all the other articles, so it would look odd to change the pattern now. Oh, and, of course, I'd like to interview you, too.'

The prospect of being interviewed usually won people round, but Strachan stiffened. 'Me?'

'I've included a profile of all the other owners who live with these superstitions,' Gisella explained. 'You're particularly interesting because you're a direct descendant of Lady Isobel.'

'Am I supposed to feel gratified that you find me so interesting?' he asked harshly. 'Why not just come out with it and say that you want to pry about my life in the same way that you want to poke around my castle?'

'It wouldn't be like that,' Gisella protested.

'Oh? What *would* it be like, then?'

'Well,' she said carefully, wondering what it was about journalists that so antagonised him, 'I'd just want to find out a bit about you, how you feel about living in a haunted—or supposedly haunted—castle, what you think about your ancestress, that kind of thing.'

'I see. And can you think of a single good reason why I should agree to all this?'

Gisella was relieved to see him looking a little less fierce. She eyed him speculatively. 'It would make an interesting piece.' Actually, she thought it would make a great piece, but she didn't want to sound too desperate.

'If you think I'm going to have my privacy invaded just to provide a few moments' interest in some rubbishy article that will be thrown away and forgotten as soon as it's read, you've got another think coming, Miss Pryde,' Strachan said flatly.

'I do not write rubbishy articles!' Gisella snapped, provoked at last into losing her temper.

'That's a matter of opinion, surely?'

'Have you ever read any of my work?' she challenged him, grey eyes cold.

'No, and I've no wish to,' he said, in the same disagreeable tone.

'It might interest you to know that I have quite a reputation as an investigative journalist,' Gisella said frostily. 'If it hadn't been for me, the Wightman scandal would never have been uncovered. The *Daily Examiner* went out on a limb to publish that story, but we were proved right in the end.'

'The *Daily Examiner*?' Strachan recoiled in disgust. 'You worked for that bunch of thugs?'

'It's a quality newspaper,' she corrected him. 'And it enjoys a very high reputation for investigative articles. If it hadn't been for the *Examiner*, hundreds of cases of exploitation or injustice would never have come to light. I worked on several of them, and I can assure you that no one who read any of those articles would claim they were "rubbishy"!'

'Could they claim they were true, though?' he sneered.

'Of course!' Gisella was outraged. 'I never write a story without researching it thoroughly.'

'The sort of research that omitted to find out my name before you came here?'

Gisella looked at him with acute dislike. 'Normally I would have found out,' she said coldly. 'But I had to do a major piece on Eric Wightman at very short notice. I simply didn't have a chance to do any research about you before I came away. I was extremely busy as it was.'

'I'm sure you were.' Strachan's lip curled. 'Journalists are always busy, busy meddling in other people's affairs, busy ruining other people's lives.'

'That's unfair!'

'Is it?' He turned back to stare down into the fire. 'I'm afraid I know to my cost how journalists work, and to what lengths they'll go to get an "interesting" story.'

The bitterness in his voice made Gisella pause, remembering suddenly what Meg had told her about his broken engagement. Had a journalist been involved in some way? It would explain his distrust of journalists.

'A beautiful girl', Meg had said. Gisella's eyes rested on the back of Strachan's neck as she wondered what his fiancée had been like. Why hadn't she married him? Was he still in love with her?

'Look.' She took a deep breath. She couldn't just give up now. 'If you don't want to be interviewed, then of course I'll respect that. I don't even need to mention your name if you'll just let me stay one night in the Candle Tower. I won't get in your way at all. You won't even know I'm there.'

Strachan looked up at that, with a glint in his dark blue eyes that Gisella found hard to interpret. 'It might be rather difficult to ignore you.'

'No, it won't. I'll stay in bed. I won't wander round snooping. I promise.'

'I see. So all you want to do is spend a night tucked up in bed in the Candle Tower?'

'Yes.' Gisella nodded eagerly. Perhaps he was going to let her stay after all?

Strachan was watching her vivid face, with its pure bone-structure. Her smooth skin was still lightly tanned from the long, hot summer and her remarkable grey eyes were imploring.

'It's very flattering, of course,' he said slowly, letting his gaze rest on the tempting curve of her mouth.

'Flattering?' Gisella was bewildered. With his eyes on her face, she was finding it difficult to concentrate. Her blood seemed to be tingling and she was very aware of his broad strength.

'Presumably you are aware that I use the Candle Tower as my bedroom? Or is this another example of your immaculate research?'

Gisella's jaw dropped ludicrously. 'Your bedroom! But it can't be!'

'Why on earth not?'

'You wouldn't sleep in a haunted room!'

Strachan stared at her in exasperation. 'We've been through all this. It's not haunted. I thought you took a scientific approach—although what's scientific about wanting to sleep with me, I'm not sure.'

'I don't want to sleep with you!' Gisella protested, flustered at the turn the conversation had taken.

'You said you wanted to spend the night in bed in the Candle Tower. That means sleeping with me. I hadn't appreciated just how far you were prepared to go to get your story!'

'You know perfectly well that I would never have suggested it if I had known it was your bedroom!'

'You wouldn't have got all dressed up if you hadn't had some kind of seduction in mind,' Strachan said unpleasantly.

'If I had seduction in mind, I certainly wouldn't be dressed like this,' Gisella snapped back, momentarily forgetting that she was dependent on his goodwill. 'This isn't my idea of a seductive outfit!'

'It's a great improvement on that ridiculous nonsense you were wearing before,' he disagreed, his eyes lingering on the soft curves of her figure. 'I must admit that I find you infinitely more desirable dressed like this.'

Gisella struggled to remain calm, but couldn't stop the wild rose flush spreading over her cheeks. 'That wasn't my intention.'

'Wasn't it?' Strachan countered cynically. 'Why change at all, then?'

'Because I——' Gisella broke off. She could hardly admit that she had hoped to charm an old man into changing his mind. 'You were the one who pointed out how inappropriate my other clothes were,' she said sulkily. 'You ought to be pleased that I took your advice.'

'Astonished would be a better word,' he said. 'I would have thought anyone who could wear pink high-heeled shoes to walk through a muddy Scottish field would be beyond advice!'

'I *had* just driven up from London,' she found herself explaining. 'They were more appropriate in a city.'

'Frankly, I find it hard to believe that pink shoes are appropriate anywhere,' Strachan said, and Gisella bristled.

'You being the great arbiter of fashion, I suppose?' she retorted. She cast a disparaging eye over his worn cords, and unexpectedly the gleam of amusement sprang back into his face.

'Fashion isn't a priority up here. Nobody cares what you look like.'

'If you don't care, why do you go on about my pink shoes?' Gisella said tartly. She didn't like the way her pulse reacted to his lurking smile.

'I'm just giving you the benefit of my advice if you want to survive a winter in Scotland.'

'I can survive perfectly well without your advice, thank you,' she said before she could help herself, and then could have kicked herself.

'You're in rather an unfortunate position, then, aren't you?' Strachan pointed out. His tone was bland, but his eyes glinted with appreciation of her dilemma. 'You can throw my opinions back in my face, but you'll never get your interview that way. As laird of Kilnacroish, I'm the only one who can give you what you claim to want so badly. The only way you'll get to spend the night in Candle Tower is sleeping with me and, attractive though you undoubtedly are, I'd just as soon sleep with a rattlesnake as a journalist!'

'The feeling's quite mutual,' Gisella snapped.

Strachan spread his hands. 'Well, that seems to settle the matter, doesn't it? I don't want you to sleep in the Candle Tower, and nor do you.'

'I do—I just don't want to sleep with you.' Gisella practically ground her teeth in frustration. 'Couldn't you move out for one night?'

'What?' Strachan stared at her as if he wondered if he had heard correctly.

'There must be dozens of bedrooms here,' Gisella said bravely. 'It seems funny to me that you *just happen* to sleep in the one I'm interested in.'

'In other words, you think I'm lying just to be obstructive?'

'Yes.' She lifted her chin and her grey eyes shone with challenge. She suspected that she had gone too far this time, but would have died rather than admit that she was nervous of his reaction.

For a long moment he just looked at her, a muscle working in his jaw, and then without warning he threw back his head and laughed. It was a deep, masculine laugh, a laugh that transformed his face with electrifying effect. Watching the grim lines dissolve so suddenly into warmth and humour, Gisella felt herself gripped by a sudden longing. She wasn't sure what it was longing for; she didn't want to know what it was longing for; she only knew that it was like a vice around her heart, widening her eyes and shortening her breath alarmingly.

'You've got a nerve, I'll give you that,' Strachan said with reluctant, exasperated admiration when he could speak. 'I've been as plain as I can be. I don't need to be obstructive; I can simply refuse you permission to do this precious article of yours, and that's what I will do. I won't do anything to help journalists. I don't want you in my house and I certainly don't want you in my bed. Anyone else would have taken the point and left by now, but all you do is calmly ask me to move out for the night!'

'*If* you really do sleep in the Candle Tower,' Gisella said, unrepentant. She had gone so far that there was no point in backing down now.

'It doesn't matter much to me whether you believe me or not, but the fact is I do. The main roof's in a terrible state and most of the bedrooms are damp. The Candle Tower, on the other hand, was renovated in the nineteenth century. It may not be very luxurious, but at least it's dry.'

'You could prove it to me just by showing me the room,' Gisella suggested. A glimpse would be enough to tell whether the room really was used as a bedroom or not.

Strachan shook his head. 'I don't need to prove anything to you, Gisella,' he pointed out. His implacable blue eyes met Gisella's resentful grey ones as he moved away from the fire and sat down in one of the comfortable-looking chairs drawn up around it. His long legs, with their stockinged feet, were stretched out in front of him, and he rested his chin on steepled fingers as he watched Gisella standing irresolute by the tray.

'The answer is no,' he went on. 'It's not a word you seem to understand, so I suggest you go and look it up in a dictionary, because my answer's not going to change.'

An odd silence fell. Strachan seemed utterly relaxed with the big dog asleep at his feet, eyebrows twitching as he dreamt. Gisella watched him, thinking hard.

She was convinced that he was bluffing, no matter what he said about the roof. Nobody in their right mind would choose to sleep in a spooky medieval tower with resident ghost when they had plenty of other bedrooms to choose from! No, he was trying to put her off.

She hadn't handled Strachan right—not that he gave the impression of a man who *could* be handled. Outside, the dusk had gathered itself into darkness, but the fire was enough to illuminate the room. Her head was bent and the blonde hair caught the flickering light and seemed to shimmer as it swung forward over her face. Suddenly she felt very tired, the frantic activity of the last few weeks in London catching up with her. She had hoped that this would be an easy article to finish off the series, but it looked as if it was going to be the most difficult of the lot. She hadn't helped by getting off on the wrong foot with Strachan McLeod either.

If it hadn't been for Yvonne's insistence, Gisella would have been tempted to have given up on the whole idea, but she knew how desperate *Focus* was for a good series of articles that would keep the reader interested from week to week. It was all very well pretending that she was a hard-hearted journalist, but she couldn't forget that Yvonne was struggling to bring up two children single-handedly, or that her editor was a notoriously ruthless man who seized on the slightest excuse to hire and fire his staff. As it was, she had promised Yvonne this article, and Gisella liked to keep her promises. Mentally, she squared her shoulders. Strachan was determined to be unhelpful, but there had to be some other way!

Deep in thought, Gisella nibbled at her thumbnail. She would just have to get into that room without Strachan knowing. He must leave the castle some time. All she had to do was slip in when no one was looking and see if his story was true. If it was indeed his bedroom, she might not be able to sleep there, but she could get a good idea of the layout and atmosphere and, if it wasn't, chances were that no one would look in there and she might well be able to spend the night without him being any the wiser.

Decision made, she looked up to surprise a strange look on Strachan's face, quickly masked.

'Well?' he asked. 'Have you remembered what "no" means yet?'

'There's no point in continuing this discussion,' Gisella said, ignoring his question. She tried to sound lofty, but suspected that the effect was suspiciously sullen.

Strachan escorted her back across the freezing expanse of the hall with what Gisella was sure was mock courtesy. 'I'm glad you've decided to be sensible and give up the whole idea,' he said as he opened the heavy oak door.

'Who said I'd given up?' Gisella said sweetly, retrieving her car keys from her bag. 'I warn you that I don't give up on a good story easily!'

Strachan looked her straight in the eyes and, involuntarily, she took a step backwards. 'And I warn *you*, Gisella, that I don't give in—at all!'

* * *

Almost exactly twenty-four hours later, Gisella sat on a log beneath the trees, and peered through the undergrowth at the castle. Strachan's Land Rover was parked on the gravel sweep and the library window was a warm yellow rectangle of light in the gloom.

Exhausted by the long drive and her confrontations with Strachan McLeod, Gisella had slept well, but the unaccustomed silence had woken her early that morning.

For a while she lay staring at the curtains, and grasping at elusive fragments of dreams floating at the edges of her consciousness. Strachan's image lingered longest: eyes, nose, jaw, the turn of his cheek, his mouth. Especially his mouth.

Gisella shifted her legs uneasily under the blankets. What was she doing, lying here, thinking about Strachan McLeod's mouth? Better by far to think about how disagreeable he had been and how she was going to get into the Candle Tower.

Swinging her legs out of bed, she went through to the kitchen and made herself a mug of coffee. She drank it standing up, shifting from foot to foot on the cold tiles while she thought about how she was going to outwit Strachan, and then rang Yvonne to let her know where she could be contacted.

'Have you got into the Candle Tower yet?' Yvonne demanded straight away.

'Have a heart! I only arrived yesterday!'

'Well, don't hang around, will you? I keep reading about the number of publications that have gone out of business this year,' she went on gloomily. 'If we don't manage to catch the readers' interest with something different soon, I'm going to be out of a job!'

Gisella rolled her eyes as she replaced the receiver. She could do without her nagging now, but she knew that Yvonne had lobbied hard for this series and, if it didn't work out, her editor would be only too pleased to offer her job to someone new.

Pulling her jacket about her now, Gisella reminded herself of Yvonne. A track led up through the woods, and she had trudged up it as dusk began to fall, anxious that Strachan should not spot her. Now she was just waiting for it to be properly dark before she explored the outside of the castle to see if there were any other entrances. The plan had been to take some notes on the atmosphere of the castle in the dark, too. She had thought about starting the article by describing how the lover must have stood in the darkness, looking up at the tower for the candle, but she hadn't counted on how spookily atmospheric the woods would be. Now she was alone in the gloom, Gisella's scepticism about ghosts wavered and, when a twig cracked near by, she jumped. Heart hammering, she crept closer to the edge of the woods and kept her eyes on the library window. The light there was a reassuring symbol of the twentieth century.

At that moment, the light went out. Gisella swallowed. She was cold, lonely and—face it—scared. 'What a great way to spend an evening!' she muttered, thinking of what she would be doing if she were in London. She might be in the wine bar for the usual post-mortem after work, or rushing home to change to go out to dinner. She might be on her way to the theatre or contemplating a self-indulgent evening at home in front of the television. She might be doing *anything* other than lurking outside a miserable Scottish castle in the dark.

The big door opened, spilling light out on to the gravel, and Gisella forgot her self-pity as Strachan appeared, followed by the faithful Bran. The big dog hesitated for a moment by the jeep, and his great head swung round as if sensing Gisella's presence. She held her breath, but at Strachan's command he jumped into the back, and the jeep's tyres crunched on the gravel as it drove off down the long avenue.

Gisella jumped to her feet. There was no need to wait for darkness now. She could have a quick scout around the castle while Strachan was away, and be safe home in her warm, unhaunted cottage in no time.

Eager to get away from the trees, she began to run over the rough grass that had once been a lawn, but momentum got the better of her. Her foot caught in a hole, and the next moment she was lying flat on her face in the wet grass.

Shaken and winded, she tried to get up, but a sharp stab of pain in her ankle made her sink back with a gasp. What a time to do something like this! And in Strachan McLeod's grounds, too! She didn't want to contemplate what he would do if he found her here. Clenching her teeth, Gisella hauled herself on to her good leg and managed to hop a couple of yards before having to stop and rest. Her ankle hurt vilely and she dropped her head between her knees to stop herself from passing out. The grass was damp and cold, and the wet seeped through her leggings, chilling her to the bone.

Struggling across the lawn a few steps at a time, Gisella soon lost track of time. For every few steps she progressed, she had to rest long minutes. She had forgotten about the article, forgotten about Yvonne. All she wanted was to be off Strachan McLeod's land before he returned.

CHAPTER FOUR

GISELLA'S luck was out.

She had almost reached the drive by the time the Land Rover came rattling round the bend, its headlights arching across the front of the castle. Numb with cold and pain, Gisella could only cower in the darkness and hope that Strachan wouldn't notice her.

He didn't, but Bran did. His barks made Strachan pause at the door, and turn slowly to see his dog standing over a huddled shape and licking it enthusiastically.

Gisella had given up as Bran found her. She collapsed back on to the grass, too tired even to fend off his licks, and closed her eyes like a child, hoping that not being able to see would make her invisible.

She could hear Strachan striding across the rough grass. He gave a smothered exclamation as he saw the limp figure for the first time. Pushing off the dog, he knelt beside her and was reaching for her wrist when Gisella opened her eyes. She had contemplated pretending to be unconscious, but somehow felt that she wouldn't be able to fool Strachan McLeod for very long.

He had a torch and was flashing it over her, but as the light caught the shimmer of blonde hair and the gleam of her eyes he let out a sigh of relief. Dropping her arm, he brought the torchlight up to rest on her white face. 'Perhaps you'd like to explain what you're doing here?' he went on, when Gisella merely looked mutinous.

'I've hurt my ankle,' she said sullenly.

'That doesn't quite answer my question, does it?'

Gisella sat up gingerly, wincing at the stab of pain from her ankle. 'I just wanted another look at the castle.'

'Oh, did you? I don't suppose it occurred to you that you were trespassing, or was this just another stroll as far as you were concerned?'

'I didn't think it would make any difference to you if I came and looked from the outside.'

'But it's dark, woman!' Strachan said, exasperated. 'You might as well have turned all the lights off and stayed at home!'

Gisella had no intention of telling him that she had planned to spy out a back entrance to the castle. 'The legend says that the candle burns in the window at night,' she said as airily as she could manage between chattering teeth. 'There's no point in coming to look for it in broad daylight.'

'There's no point in coming to look for it at all,' Strachan said acidly. 'How many times do I have to tell you? It's just a story.'

'I'm well aware of that,' Gisella said, trying to hang on to some semblance of dignity. 'I wasn't exactly expecting to see a candle! I was just trying to absorb some atmosphere.' It was the truth, if not the whole truth. 'I can't possibly write the article unless I've done that—and preferably seen the Candle Tower as well.'

Strachan rolled his eyes. 'Only you would have the nerve to try and nag me when you're cold and wet and hurt and I've just caught you trespassing!' He shook his head as he looked at her. 'I'd have thought you'd have realised that I'm not the sympathetic type, Gisella. You'll have to make do with describing the atmosphere from outside. God knows, you must have absorbed enough of it while you've been lying here! You're lucky Bran spotted you, or you'd have been here all night. I hope you're grateful to him.'

Gisella glanced at the dog. He was sitting on his haunches, tail wagging surreptitiously. If it hadn't been for him, Strachan would never have known she was here.

'Just at this moment, I don't feel very grateful,' she said a little childishly.

'You should do. I wouldn't be surprised if it freezes tonight. You could have had a bad case of exposure.' He grimaced as the drizzle in the torchlight turned to light, ominous rain, and turned back to Gisella with an irritable sigh. 'We'd better get you inside.'

'I'll be all right,' said Gisella, a stubborn set to her jaw. 'I don't want to invade your precious privacy again.'

'Don't be stupid, Gisella.' Strachan spoke as if to a child. 'It's going to pour in a minute.' Straightening, he bent down to help her up. His hand was strong and not ungentle beneath her elbow, and she was glad of his firm grip as she balanced uneasily on one foot.

'You're not going to get very far like that, are you?' He regarded her with some annoyance and, before Gisella knew what was happening, he had hoisted her over his shoulder in a fireman's lift and was striding towards the door, with Bran trotting beside him.

Dangling over his shoulder in the least dignified of positions, Gisella gritted her teeth with humiliation. She was very conscious of his arm like a piece of solid oak against the back of her knees, but he carried her as if she were of no more interest than a sack of potatoes.

The library was lit only by the glow of the dying fire as Strachan shouldered open the door and dumped her in an armchair. Never had a room looked so warm and welcoming! He turned away to switch on a table lamp before throwing a couple of logs on the fire and stirring the flames back into life.

'You need to get warm,' he said gruffly, with a glance at Gisella's white, set face. Her grey eyes looked enormous as she huddled in the chair, still numb with cold and tense with embarrassment. 'You'd better get out of those clothes for a start.'

'I don't think——' she began, but he interrupted.

'Believe me, Gisella, seduction is the last thing on my mind, if that's what you're worried about,' he said. 'For once in your life, why don't you try and think sensibly? You need to get warm and dry, and I can't do anything about your ankle until you are.' He headed for the door before Gisella had a chance to reply. 'I'll go and find you something to preserve your modesty.'

He shut the door, leaving Gisella to glower after him in frustration. The worst thing was knowing he was right! She was shivering as she bent to pull the fashionable ankle-high boot off her good foot. The suede was sodden and she grimaced as she dropped it to the floor. Now for the other one...

When Strachan came back with a thick towelling robe over his arm, he found her whiter than ever, her face screwed up, and gasping in pain as she tried to ease the boot over her swollen ankle.

'What are you doing?' He was across the room in two strides, snatching her hands away from her boot. 'Are you some kind of masochist? We're going to have to cut it off.'

'Oh, no!' Gisella whimpered. 'Not my Italian boots!'

'Well, we could always cut your foot off if you want to save the boot,' Strachan suggested caustically. He pulled a pair of heavy-duty scissors out of his jacket pocket. 'I thought we'd need these.' He hooked a battered pouffe forwards with his foot and sat down in front of her chair. 'Give me your foot,' he ordered, pushing up the sleeves of his jumper to reveal strong forearms covered in fine dark hairs.

Reluctantly, Gisella extended her leg, and he rested it across his knee while he cut expertly through the suede. 'I bought those in Milan,' she said sadly, and then winced as he eased her badly swollen ankle free.

'You seem to have a thing about frivolous footwear,' Strachan commented, regarding the ruined boot with disgust. 'It beats me why anyone would pay good money for anything quite so useless. Turquoise suede boots! What use are they to anybody?'

'They were very comfortable,' Gisella said, on the defensive. 'I wore them a lot.'

Strachan snorted. 'If you're planning to stay here, I suggest you buy yourself some proper gumboots. Pink shoes and turquoise boots are all very well in a city, but they won't get you very far in the country.'

'So you keep saying!' Gisella said sulkily.

'Some proper clothes would be sensible too,' he continued remorselessly. 'How on earth did you expect to keep warm in *these*?' He plucked at her sodden green leggings in disbelief and shook his head over her bright blue sweatshirt. 'And just a thin jacket over the top!'

'I thought I'd have a quick look and go straight home,' Gisella pointed out, ruffled. 'I didn't expect to spend hours lying on your wet grass.'

'Well, whose fault is that?'

'I caught my foot in a rabbit hole. Your lawn's absolutely riddled with them,' she grumbled. 'Why don't you mow it?'

'Keeping my grass mown so that trespassers don't fall down rabbit holes is not one of my priorities at the moment,' Strachan said in a scathing tone. 'I haven't got time to do half the things that need to be done urgently.'

Gisella watched him covertly as he picked up the tattered boot and the scissors and stood up. For the first time she noticed the lines of tiredness around his eyes, and she wondered about the circumstances that had left him struggling alone with the remnants of what had obviously been a wealthy estate.

'I'll leave you to take your clothes off,' he said briskly, heading for the door.

'Bet you say that to all the girls,' Gisella muttered, but subsided when he shot her a look.

All he said was, 'I'll go and find a bandage.'

As soon as he had gone, she wriggled awkwardly out of her wet things, hung them over the fireguard and hopped back to the chair to wrap herself in the blissfully dry towelling robe. It was soft and worn and she wondered if it was Strachan's. The thought made her flush with awareness.

Bran had been watching her from the hearth with his steady brown eyes. As she settled back into the chair, he padded over and threw himself down beside her, resting his head against her knee with a sigh. Gisella looked down at him with a rueful smile. It was hard to resist an animal who was determined to like you.

'I don't really like dogs,' she said, trying to sound discouraging, but her hand stroked his wiry head. Bran's eyes half closed with pleasure and he heaved another contented sigh. 'I suppose you're quite nice, really,' she went on, fondling his ear. 'At least you're friendly, not like your master.'

'I see you've got yourself a chaperon.' Strachan's dry voice came from the doorway, and she jumped, blushing as she realised that he must have overheard her. 'I've never seen him act like this before,' he went on as he came into the room, shutting the door behind him to keep out the dank chill of the hall. 'He seems utterly besotted with you. He's usually more discerning.'

'There's no accounting for taste,' Gisella said, a trifle sourly.

Strachan shifted the pouffe slightly nearer the chair and patted his knee to indicate that she should rest her leg on it. After a moment's hesitation, Gisella obeyed, but she was very conscious of the length of bare leg, and wrapped the robe firmly over her knee where it threatened to flap open. Strachan shot her a sardonic look but made no comment.

He took her slim calf in his hand and explored the swollen ankle with gentle fingers. His touch was quite impersonal, but Gisella was excruciatingly aware of his strong, hard hands. They were farmer's hands, tough and calloused and reassuringly capable, and her skin seemed to burn beneath them. If they were this disturbing against her foot, what would it be like if they slid upwards, smoothing over her leg and hard against the softness of her thigh?

Gisella gave an involuntary gasp at the thought, and Strachan looked up quickly.

'Did that hurt?'

'A little,' she said in a husky voice. Her ankle did throb uncomfortably.

'It's badly swollen, but there's nothing broken. I'll strap it up, and it should be fine in a few days.'

'Thank you,' she said, a little awkwardly. His head was bent as he picked up the bandage from the carpet and began to wrap it carefully around her foot, and all she could see was the cool, hard line of his cheek and the ucompromising set of his jaw.

The brush of his fingers against her skin was doing strange things to Gisella's pulse. She fought to keep it under control, but when he slipped his hand beneath her calf to shift it slightly she was unable to prevent a shiver of response at his touch.

Strachan must have felt her quiver, for he glanced up at her face. Horribly self-conscious, unable to meet his eyes, she stared fixedly down at Bran, but she could feel his gaze drop to her exposed knee, and down her slender leg to the angry swelling of her ankle and the elegant foot with its immaculately painted toenails.

From beneath her lashes, Gisella saw him shake his head as he rubbed his thumb across a bright pink nail.

'Don't tell me!' she cried, before he had a chance to make some sarcastic comment. 'Painted toenails aren't appropriate for the country?'

'You're learning,' said Strachan unpleasantly, and resumed his bandaging. His hands were deft as they twisted the bandage firmly around her foot and up around her ankle for support. 'I have to admit that I can't see the point.' He glanced at her face again, and for a moment his hands stilled as his eyes rested on her mouth. 'Did you really put lipstick on just to walk through the woods?' he asked, turning away abruptly.

'Why shouldn't I?'

'You didn't expect to meet anyone, did you?'

'I met you,' she pointed out.

'I'm afraid it would take a lot more than a dash of lipstick to make me change my opinion of you.'

'You surprise me!' said Gisella with heavy irony. 'Anyway, what you think is beside the point.'

'Oh? What *is* the point, then?'

'My self-esteem,' she said promptly. 'I'd feel naked if I didn't have any make-up on.'

'And how did your self-esteem react when you fell down a rabbit hole?'

Gisella shot him a look of dislike. 'Why are people in the country always so superior? What does it matter whether I wear lipstick or not? I wear it in London, so I'll wear it here. I have this theory that country people feel intimidated by any hint of sophistication. Everyone looks askance if you don't conform down to your wellington boots.'

'What a load of rubbish!' Strachan snorted.

'It's true. Why else would you make such a fuss about my shoes?'

'If you think you intimidate me, you've got another think coming,' said Strachan, tying the ends of the bandage in a neat knot. 'And I can assure you that you don't look all that sophisticated at the moment, either!'

His words brought Gisella up short and she looked down at her hands. They were filthy from pulling herself along the grass, and she hated to think what her hair looked like. She felt it gingerly. It was wet and tangled.

'Don't look so horrified!' Strachan stood up, replacing her leg carefully back on the pouffe. 'It's not the end of the world if you don't look as if you've stepped out of a glossy magazine.' He poured two glasses of whisky, and came back across the room to thrust one into her hand. 'In fact, I'm not sure I don't prefer you like this.'

The breath dried in Gisella's throat as their eyes met, and for a moment they stared at each other before Strachan turned away. He sat in the armchair on the other side of the fire and gazed down into his whisky, turning the glass slowly between his hands. The light from the blazing fire flickered over his face, softening the harsh features. A tense silence fell.

Why was her heart suddenly thudding like this? It hadn't been much of a compliment, but there had been a strange look in Strachan's eyes as he looked down at her. Gisella stared desperately down into her own glass, but her eyes kept sliding to the angular cheekbones and the inflexible set of his jaw. His mouth was a firm, cool line and, deep within her, something stirred disquietingly, clenching the base of her spine.

It was very quiet except for the hiss and crackle of the burning logs. Strachan looked abstracted, remote and self-contained in the reflected firelight. A frown creased between his brows, and Gisella wondered what he was thinking about. How many evenings did he sit like this, alone with Bran? Did he worry about the estate, about the castle crumbling about him? It would be easy enough to forget about them in this warm, comfortable room, Gisella reflected as her thoughts drifted. She pulled mindlessly on Bran's ear, and he gave a rumbling sigh of appreciation without opening his eyes. You could pull the faded velvet curtains, like now, and shut out the rest of the world, especially if you had someone with you, someone you loved...

Appalled at the train of her thoughts, Gisella took a gulp of her whisky without thinking and promptly choked as it burnt down her throat.

'Steady on!' said Strachan disapprovingly. 'That's my best malt.'

At least it had broken the silence. Strachan no longer looked remote. He just looked tired and irritable.

'Feeling any warmer?'

Warm? She had been feeling positively hot! 'Yes, thank you,' she said meekly.

'Do you realise what a stupid thing you did in coming out dressed like that? What do you think would have happened if Bran hadn't found you?'

'I'd have got home somehow,' she said, recovering her old defiance.

'You could have died of exposure,' he said grimly, ignoring her. 'Next time you go trespassing, wear some warm clothes.'

Gisella sighed. 'I don't make a habit of twisting my ankle.'

'Tell me, is this article of yours really worth all this effort?' he asked. 'You've had to hang around in the dark, you practically froze to death, and you won't be able to walk properly for a few days. The story can't be that important! Why don't you just take no for an answer and give up?'

'I can't give up,' said Gisella. 'I've been commissioned to write this series, and I can't let the magazine down. Other people are relying on me, and if I don't produce what I said I would then I won't get another commission. I've only just started as a freelance, so I can't afford to get a reputation as being unreliable. Quite apart from anything else,' she went on, 'once a story gets to you, you just can't let it go. I want to know what it is about the Candle Tower that gives it such superstition, and I will.'

'And if I say you can't?'

'I'll find out somehow,' she said stubbornly.

Strachan's lips curled in disgust. 'Like a dog worrying a bone! Why do you do it?'

'I've told you.' Gisella shrugged. 'It's my job, and I want to do it well.'

'Something more than that must drive you,' Strachan said. 'Don't you want anything else? You must want more than just to do your job well. Don't you want marriage? Children?'

Gisella looked into the fire. 'Yes, one day. I've just never met anyone I wanted to marry. Perhaps I never gave anyone a proper chance, but for the last few years I've made journalism my priority.' She paused reflectively. 'I suppose what I really want is security.'

'Security seems an odd thing for a girl like you to want,' he commented, as if he was curious despite himself.

'I've only got myself to rely on,' Gisella said. 'My parents were killed in a car crash when I was seventeen, and there wasn't any money, just memories. I threw myself into getting a degree and then a job, as something to hang on to. Having a career was my security.' She hesitated, wondering why she was telling Strachan McLeod all this, but something made her go on. 'When you're on your own, having your own place becomes really important, too. At least, it did to me. I worked hard to earn enough to buy my little flat, so now I've got that as security and I'm independent. I loved being a reporter. It's exhilarating working on a paper and being ready to drop everything and rush off at a moment's notice, but I was beginning to get tired. I want to try writing a novel, and going freelance gives me the freedom to do that now that I've got my flat to fall back on if it doesn't work out.'

She glanced over at Strachan to find him watching her with a strange expression, as if he had glimpsed something of the vulnerable girl beneath the shell of independence and sophistication she had built about her.

'I know what it's like to be on your own,' he said quietly, 'and I know how important a home is, too. Oh, I know I didn't have to work to buy mine,' he said, catching her look, 'but I've had to work bloody hard to keep it. You inherit the responsibility as well as the expense, and you don't have any choice about it.'

'You could always sell it,' Gisella said, even though she found it impossible to imagine Strachan in any other setting.

'No,' he said flatly. 'It was touch and go at the beginning, but I've fought too long to keep the castle to give up now.'

It was obvious how much this cold, crumbling building meant to him, and Gisella sensed that he didn't open up like this very often. 'Do you really sleep in the Candle Tower?' she asked on impulse.

'Yes.' The dark blue eyes gleamed with the by now familiar combination of exasperation and amusement.

'Don't you ever think about what must have happened in that room?' She leant forward eagerly. 'After all, Isobel was your ancestress. You must feel *something* of her there.'

'Is this an interview?' Strachan countered, the sardonic note back in his voice.

'No.' Gisella looked at him with direct grey eyes. 'You said you didn't want to be interviewed, so I won't. But... well, I'm interested. I think if I slept there, I'd always be thinking about Isobel. Not as a ghost,' she added hastily. 'Just trying to imagine what she must have felt. She must have been so cold and lonely.'

'And so disloyal,' Strachan finished harshly. 'I'm afraid I don't have much sympathy to waste on faithless women.' He looked so bleak that Gisella was sure, with a sharp twinge of something almost like jealousy, that he must be thinking of his broken engagement.

'I hadn't thought of it like that before,' she said carefully. 'She's always portrayed as a heroine in the versions I've read.'

'Yes, poor Isobel,' Strachan mocked. 'Poor, rich, beautiful Isobel, with nothing better to do with her time than cuckold her husband and tempt another man to his doom!'

'Perhaps she really loved him,' suggested Gisella. 'She must have done to have taken such risks.'

'Is that what you think love is, Gisella? Playing games with a man's life? It was a game to her, putting the candle in the window, letting him take all the risk of being caught outside. If she'd loved him, she'd have left him alone.' He drained his whisky and set the glass down on the floor. 'It's an old story. Why are you so interested in it?'

'I'm not sure,' Gisella admitted. 'It's about love and death and betrayal. They're all universal themes.'

'You don't need to go back to the fourteenth century to find a story about love, death and betrayal,' Strachan said bitterly. 'There's plenty of that in the twentieth century.'

She looked at him warily, wondering what he was thinking about with such bitterness. 'I'm really just interested in how stories like that acquire ghosts,' she said after a pause. 'At what point do they stop being history and start being fantasy? I'm sure it can be logically explained if you explore the site thoroughly——' She broke off as Strachan shook his head with an air of finality.

'If this is designed to get you into the tower, Gisella, you might as well save your breath,' he said. 'As far as I'm concerned it's just a bedroom, and I don't propose to allow it to be described in detail just for the entertainment of your readers.'

'But they wouldn't know it's your bedroom——'

'I said *no*.'

'It would be so easy to get rid of me by just letting me have a look,' she pleaded. 'Just a peek?'

'It would be even easier by kicking you out my front door,' he pointed out unpleasantly. 'Which is what I will do if you're not careful!'

Gisella sighed. Strachan's intransigence was making her itch with curiosity. Just getting to the tower had taken on the nature of a challenge now. 'Don't worry, I'll go,' she said loftily. 'But could I use your loo first?' If she had a few minutes to herself, she might be able to sneak a quick look around.

Strachan escorted her across the glacial stone hall and down a corridor, Gisella leaning heavily on his arm. 'There are some walking sticks behind the door,' he said as he showed her into a room bigger than her bedroom in the London flat.

'Oh, fine,' she said casually. 'Well, don't wait in the cold. I'll come back to the library.' She grinned as she closed the door. Perfect! Quickly she struggled back into her clothes, which had practically dried in front of the fire.

The room seemed far too grand for its purpose. It was hung with dark red wallpaper covered with shooting prints, and Gisella needed a walking stick just to get across to the antiquated lavatory, where she pulled the chain for effect. The resultant roar practically deafened her, and she viewed the shuddering cistern with some alarm. The last thing she wanted was Strachan banging on the door demanding to know what she had done to the plumbing. It seemed to know what it was doing, though, so she limped back to the door.

Putting her ear to the wood, she tried to hear if Strachan was lurking outside, but the door was solid and, in any case, she would be lucky to hear anything over the noise of the cistern, which was filling up with a lot of self-important rumbling.

Very cautiously, Gisella opened the door a crack and squinted up and down the corridor. All seemed to be clear. Strachan must have gone back to the library after all.

Slipping out of the door, she turned and began hobbling as fast as she could towards the stone staircase at the end of the corridor. She was almost there when a dry voice spoke behind her.

'The library's this way, Gisella.'

Gisella stopped dead with a frustrated sigh. She turned round slowly. Strachan was leaning against the arch which led into the hall. His arms were folded and his face was alive with malicious amusement.

'It's just as well I hung around in case you lost your way,' he said with obvious irony. 'It's easy to get disorientated with all these doors.'

Gisella eyed him with deep resentment as she limped back towards him. 'You should put up notices if you don't want people wandering around,' she said sulkily.

'Most people are welcome to look around,' Strachan said as she came up to him. 'It's only certain people I object to.'

She ignored that. 'In that case, why don't you open the castle to the public?' she asked as they recrossed the echoing hall. 'That would bring in some money, wouldn't it?'

'Some, but this part of Scotland isn't on the tourist trail. I doubt if we'd get many visitors, at least not enough to justify all the work I'd have to do just to make it fit to be seen.'

'You wouldn't have to do much,' Gisella said. 'It's romantic enough as it is.'

Strachan opened the library door for her. 'That's the second time you've talked about romance. I always thought journalists were the least romantic of people.'

'I'm not romantic,' said Gisella, trying to sound brisk. 'But other people are. Lots of them would probably love to stay in a crumbling old castle like this.'

'So you think I should take in paying guests, do you?'

'Why not? It positively reeks of history. Even the loo's an antique!'

Strachan gave one of his devastating, unexpected grins and, as once before, Gisella found herself dangerously unprepared for its effect. 'It's a work of art, isn't it? It takes at least an hour for the cistern to fill up. I don't think the guests would be very impressed by the plumbing.'

'You could always sell yourself as being the most uncomfortable holiday available anywhere,' Gisella suggested, having got her breathing back under control. 'I'm sure lots of people would love it. You know... you too can shiver all weekend, sleep in a damp room, bring your own bucket to catch the rain dripping through the roof, special supplement for haunted rooms... that kind of thing.'

'And then there's my cooking... It could be a memorable weekend!'

They both laughed, and then their eyes met and they both stopped laughing abruptly, as if they remembered at the same time that they weren't supposed to like each other.

CHAPTER FIVE

An awkward silence fell, broken only by Bran's snoring. He lay sprawled on the hearthrug, ignoring them. Gisella was suddenly very conscious of Strachan's massive strength. She wished he would laugh again.

'I—er—I ought to phone for a taxi,' she said.

'There's no need for that. I'll take you home.'

Strachan sounded oddly angry, and Gisella's own voice sharpened, more in reaction to the way her heart had soared as he laughed than to his brusqueness.

'You mean you want to escort me off the premises?'

'At least that way I'll know you've gone!'

Renewed antagonism jangled between them on the silent ride back to the cottage. Strachan jumped out without speaking and would have lifted her bodily out of the Land Rover if Gisella had not protested.

'Come on, Gisella!' he said impatiently. 'You've wasted enough of my evening already!' He hoisted her out without ceremony, and Gisella was forced to put her arms round his neck. Her face was very close to his, and she looked determinedly over his shoulder as he carried her up to the door and tried to open it.

'It's locked,' she informed him in a tight voice, trying to keep her racing pulse under control.

'Very sensible,' said Strachan. 'You never know who's going to come snooping round your home, do you?' Their eyes clashed for a moment, but Gisella was the first to look away. 'Have you got the key?' he asked, studiously patient.

Sulkily, Gisella retrieved it from her jacket pocket and handed it over. Still holding her, Strachan unlocked the door, kicked it open and carried her inside, switching on the light with his elbow. He set her down on her good foot, but kept a steadying arm about her as she found her balance.

'At least with that ankle you won't be tempted to go wandering around anywhere else tonight,' he said dourly.

They were standing close together, and suddenly Gisella's heart was beating so loudly that she was sure he must be able to hear it. Part of her mind screamed at her to step away from him, to thank him politely and wish him a firm goodnight. The other noted how safe and strong his arm felt, how broad his chest was, and how, if he tightened his arm just fractionally, she would be able to lean against him.

Her mouth was dry as, almost against her will, she lifted her head. Strachan was staring down at her, his blue eyes dark and impossible to read. For one wild, breathless moment she felt his arm tense as if he was about to pull her to him, but then it dropped and he stepped back abruptly.

'I'd better get back,' he said, and the next moment he had gone, closing the door behind him with a half-angry snap and leaving Gisella staring at where he had been.

It was a long time before she was able to sleep that night. She shifted restlessly, thumping her pillow, tossing the eiderdown on to the floor and then heaving it back on to the bed, but it was impossible to get comfortable.

She told herself that it was because her ankle hurt, or that she was used to sleeping under a duvet instead of these heavy blankets, but deep down she knew it was something else. The memory of Strachan's dark blue eyes and the disquieting gleam of his smile burned up and down her mind.

Gisella turned on to her side and tried to find a comfortable spot on the pillow. He was brusque and disagreeable, he hated journalists, he wouldn't let her stay in the Candle Tower, he thought she was stupid and annoying . . . why had she felt so at home sitting in the warm library with the sleeping dog at her feet? She had never liked dour men and she had never liked dogs. Why did she wish she hadn't spoilt everything by remembering that she was a journalist?

She threw herself over on to her other side, pulling the sheet tightly around her. She was a journalist. She wanted to get into the castle to write her article, that was all. Once it was done, she wouldn't care if she never saw Strachan or his big, soppy dog again.

By the time morning came, she had convinced herself. Her ankle was still sore and swollen, but she was anxious to find out more about the history of Kilnacroish Castle, so she rang Meg and persuaded her to drive her into Crieston. As the county town, it was bound to have a library, and she wanted to see what she could find in the local history section.

Meg was always willing to go shopping, and she picked Gisella up a couple of hours later, with many exclamations when she saw her bandaged foot.

'How on earth did you do that?'

'Oh, I was just out for a walk,' Gisella said vaguely.

Meg watched the way she limped to the car, leaning on a walking stick. 'You never walked back to the cottage?'

'Someone gave me a lift.' Gisella made a great fuss of settling herself in the car and wedging the stick neatly between her knees, but Meg was not to be diverted.

'Who?'

Gisella gave in, and told her friend what had happened. Admittedly, it was an edited version, which omitted her own confused reactions to Strachan and the abortive attempt to find the Candle Tower by herself, but for some reason Gisella decided to keep those to herself.

Meg clucked over the accident, but was none the less impressed. 'After that letter he sent you, I'm surprised he didn't come after you with a shotgun! What's he like?'

'He's insufferable,' said Gisella with a smouldering eye, remembering some of the things he had said to her. 'He was very disagreeable about the whole thing!'

'I wouldn't have said that picking you up, bandaging your foot, pouring whisky down you and then driving you home was exactly disagreeable!' Meg commented as she started the car.

'You don't know what he was like,' Gisella said sulkily. 'He wasn't exactly charming! He's anti-journalists and anti-women, so you can imagine what he thought of me!'

'He can't have thought you were that bad, or he wouldn't have looked after you like that.'

'He just wanted to get rid of me as quickly as possible, that's all. He made it very clear that he didn't like me, and he's got no intention of letting me anywhere near the Candle Tower!' Gisella glowered through the windscreen. The hills were a purplish blue today, beneath a bright sky.

'Is he attractive?'

'He's all right, I suppose, if you like that dour Scottish look. He's not my type.'

'Well, go on! That doesn't tell me very much!'

Gisella sighed. 'There isn't anything else to tell. He's just dark and grim.'

'Eyes?'

'Blue . . . dark blue.' She fingered the walking stick, remembering. 'There's nothing particularly special about him.'

'In other words, you really fell for him!' Meg said, with a sideways glance at Gisella's face.

'No, I didn't!' Gisella said crossly. 'I've told you, he's not at all my type.' She glared at Meg, who merely smiled blandly at the road ahead. 'There's absolutely no danger of me falling for Strachan

McLeod,' she asserted, but her voice sounded weak and uncertain even to her own ears.

Gisella was glad when Meg dropped her at the library and arranged to pick her up later. She wanted to concentrate on what she was doing, and it was easier to remember that she was a cool, professional journalist without her friend around. Sometimes she thought that Meg knew her a little too well for comfort!

A helpful librarian pointed her in the right direction, and she soon forgot about Meg, as she pored over the local histories, absorbed in fitting the various pieces of information together. There were several different versions of Isobel's story, but the basic elements were the same: Isobel and her lover and the mysterious candle which people claimed still burned in her window, beckoning him on.

Gisella looked up from the books and stared absently at the wall. Isobel was an elusive character. Had she been a reckless, passionate woman, reckoning the world well lost for love, or was she as treacherous and spoilt as Strachan had claimed?

Strachan.

Absorbed in the fourteenth century, she was unprepared for the jolt of memory. She could picture him so clearly: the strong, aggressive features, the tough body, the unsettling mouth with its rare, reluctant smile.

Gisella forced her gaze back down to the book in front of her, but she turned the next few pages mindlessly until suddenly she realised that she was staring down at a plan of Castle Kilnacroish.

It was exactly what she needed.

The castle rooms were neatly marked on the plan and, most important of all, there, on the corner, was the Isobel Tower, clearly labelled. Gisella studied the layout carefully, trying to relate it to what she had seen the night before. There was the library, there the stone staircase she had tried so hard to reach. It was nowhere near the tower! There were so many rooms, so many twisting staircases and confusing corridors that she would need the map if she was ever to get another chance to look round.

She made several copies of the plan on the library photocopier and, satisfied with her morning's work, handed back the books and headed towards the swing doors.

It was still quite early, she realised, hesitating in the dingy entrance hall. Home-made posters for local events were pinned on the wall between more official notices and instructions. An elderly lady was standing helplessly in front of the mass of information, as if wondering where to start.

Gisella glanced at her watch and decided that there was time for her to have a cup of coffee before she had to meet Meg, but as she limped past the old lady she couldn't help noticing the red eyes and tremulous mouth.

'Can I help you at all?' she asked gently, unable to simply ignore her. 'It's probably none of my business, but you look upset. Is there anything I can do?'

She wondered at first if the old lady had even heard her. Her face was drawn and the faded blue eyes were desperately worried. In one arthritic hand, she clutched a damp handkerchief.

'I don't know,' she quavered. 'I don't know where to begin...oh, dear, what am I going to do?'

'Are you looking for some information?' Gisella asked patiently.

'I wondered if there might be a lawyer...but Archie says we won't be able to afford it, and then what will we do for money? He says we'll just have to accept it.' She twisted the handkerchief in her hands, and Gisella's heart was touched by her obvious distress.

'I'm sure we'll be able to find someone to help you,' she said. 'Can you tell me exactly what the problem is?'

The old lady turned to her, clearly relieved to find someone who seemed prepared to listen. 'It's the house,' she explained tremulously. 'They want to turn us out of our house, and Archie's crippled. Where will we go?' The wrinkled face looked up at Gisella in despair.

Gisella frowned in concern, but it was possible that the old lady had misunderstood the situation. 'Look,' she said in a practical voice. 'Why don't you let me buy you a cup of tea, and you can tell me all about it? I'm a reporter, and if I can't help you I'll find someone who can,' she promised.

'Oh, I'd be so grateful if you could!'

'Let's go, then,' said Gisella. 'You can explain everything when we've got some tea but, I warn you, you'll have to help me across the road!'

She nodded down at her bandaged ankle, and the old lady laughed a little shakily as she took

Gisella's arm. Somehow or another they got themselves into a tea-shop, and by the time they had settled themselves she was looking calmer and was able to tell her story without the threatened tears.

Her name was Ailsa Donald, she told Gisella, and she and her husband Archie had been tenants in the same cottage for forty-seven years. Archie had been crippled in a farm accident some years ago, but they had always been careful tenants and it had never occurred to them that they might have to leave. Until yesterday, that was, when, out of the blue, they had had a letter from the agent telling them that they would have to find somewhere else to live as the cottage was about to be demolished.

'Did he give any reason?' Gisella asked.

'"Unsafe", he said, but it's not unsafe. We've been living there, and we should know! I told him that too,' Mrs Donald remembered, and Gisella was glad to see her distress had given way to indignation. 'But he just said that he'd been given orders to evict us as soon as possible. Just doing his job, he said!'

Gisella looked thoughtful. 'Who owns the cottage?'

'We've always been part of the Kilnacroish estate,' Mrs Donald said sadly. 'Nothing like this has ever happened before.'

So Strachan McLeod was behind this! 'Leave it to me, Mrs Donald,' Gisella said, sitting up straight. He had no business treating an elderly couple like this, and she would make sure he knew it. She would positively enjoy putting a spoke in *his* wheel for a change!

She told Meg what she had learnt about Strachan as they drove back to the cottage. 'What a heartless thing to do,' said Meg, suitably indignant. 'But there isn't anything you can do, is there?'

'There's *always* something you can do,' Gisella said. 'And for a start I'm going to tell Strachan McLeod exactly what I think of him!'

'Giving him a good ticking off isn't likely to get you into his castle,' Meg pointed out practically, but Gisella's blood was up.

'I don't care! I can't just sit back and let him bully a defenceless old couple.'

As they drew up outside the cottage, Gisella stiffened. Strachan was just closing the gate into the bullocks' field, but at the sound of the car he turned, a tall, dark, forbidding figure with the huge dog by his side. At the first sight of him, Gisella's heart had lurched alarmingly, and she took a steadying breath as she reached for the handle.

'That's him,' she said to Meg. 'I'm going to tackle him right now!'

Meg's eyes widened as she looked at Strachan, and she glanced back at Gisella a little doubtfully. 'He looks awfully tough.'

'I'm not afraid of Strachan McLeod!' Gisella's eyes held a militant sparkle.

'If you give me the key, I'll go and put the kettle on,' said Meg in a cowardly way. 'I don't want to get caught in the crossfire!'

Gisella hardly heard her. She was marching over to Strachan, but the impression of cold professionalism she had hoped to create was spoilt by Bran, who bounded over and insisted on greeting her with slavish adoration. By the time she had pushed him aside, she was looking pink and ruffled from his enthusiastic licks.

'Can't you keep your dog under control?' she demanded crossly.

'He's got some kind of psychological disorder,' Strachan explained. 'He likes you.' He shook his head at the strangeness of it all.

Gisella's lips tightened. 'I'm glad I met you,' she said in a cold voice. 'I was coming to see you this afternoon.'

'You're always coming to see me, Gisella,' Strachan said with a sigh. 'And my answer is always the same—no. Why won't you accept that?'

A cold wind was blowing, and Gisella wrapped her peacock-blue cardigan more closely about her. She wished she'd got her jacket out of the back of the car. 'I don't want to talk about staying in the castle,' she said.

'Well, that makes a pleasant change! I didn't know you had another topic of conversation.' Strachan turned back to check the fastening on the gate. 'What *did* you want to see me about?'

'I want to know why you're throwing a defenceless old couple out of their cottage!'

'I beg your pardon?'

'Don't try to deny it! I was told all about it.' Gisella tucked her hair defiantly behind her ears.

Strachan stared at her. 'I don't know what you're talking about.'

'I suppose you don't know about any eviction order, either?'

'No, I don't.' He was beginning to sound exasperated. 'Perhaps if you explained a little more clearly, it might make it easier to decide what it is I do or don't know?'

'All right.' Gisella took her notebook from the pocket of her cardigan and flicked through to the notes she had made when talking to Mrs Donald. 'I met a Mrs Donald today. She was very distressed because she and her husband have had notice to leave the cottage they've lived in for...' she consulted her notes '...forty-seven years. Is any of this sounding familiar yet? They've been told that it's to be demolished, regardless of the fact that they'll find it difficult to find anywhere else to go. Archie Donald is crippled and——'

'Archie Donald?' he interrupted her.

'So you do know them!'

'Of course I know Archie,' Strachan said with a touch of irritation. 'Donald's a common name around here. I didn't realise you meant Ailsa and Archie. He used to work for my father before his accident. What's all this about their being evicted?'

Gisella lifted her chin in challenge. 'You tell me!'

'How should I know?' he snapped. 'You seem to be the one with all the information round here!'

'Mrs Donald told me their cottage was part of the Kilnacroish estate. I presume that makes them your tenants?'

Strachan stuck his hands in the pockets of his jacket and looked at her with dislike. 'You presume wrong, then, Gisella. I'm sure Mrs Donald still thinks of the cottage as being part of the estate, but I had to sell a large part of it a couple of years ago. A number of cottages had to go, including this one and the Donalds'.'

Gisella heard him out with a sinking feeling. 'Oh,' she said, deflated.

'You may have had me down as the wicked landlord,' he went on, 'but I'm afraid I have to disappoint you. I'd suggest that you check your facts before you run around making wild accusations like that—or is this yet more evidence of your famous lack of research?'

'I had no reason to disbelieve Mrs Donald,' she muttered. 'She *told* me they were Kilnacroish tenants.' Even as she spoke, she remembered that that was not exactly what Mrs Donald had said, and she cursed herself for not checking. She had been too eager to find that Strachan McLeod was in the wrong.

'She probably thinks they still are,' Strachan was saying. 'The change of ownership made very little difference to the tenants. They still pay their rent to the same agent. Just because somebody tells you something doesn't mean that it's true, any more than being published in a paper makes a story true. I'd have thought you'd have known that. You don't look the naïve type.'

Gisella gritted her teeth. 'I'm sorry if I jumped to the wrong conclusion.' She was damned if she was going to grovel to him! 'Look, who did you sell the land to?'

'What business is it of yours?' he asked, dark blue eyes hostile and mouth set in an angry line.

'If it's not you, then I want to find out who *is* responsible for this eviction order.'

'Why? What's it got to do with you?'

'It isn't anything to do with me, other than the fact that I saw an old lady crying this morning and I said I'd help her,' Gisella said fiercely. 'I can't let an elderly couple be turfed out of their home if there's something I can do to prevent it, can I?'

'I'd have thought a lawyer would be more useful,' Strachan said dampeningly, and Gisella's eyes flashed.

'Lawyers cost money, and I wouldn't be surprised if the owners are legally within their rights. A story in the local paper getting public opinion on the Donalds' side is likely to be much more effective.'

'And, as an added bonus, Gisella Pryde gets another story in the paper?'

'This is hardly going to be a world exclusive,' she snapped. 'I just think that too many elderly people get taken advantage of because they're old and confused. Someone's hoping that the Donalds will just accept the eviction without a fight. They're hoping they won't begin to know where to look for help. Well, as luck would have it, Mrs Donald found me, and I'm not going to let them be treated unfairly.' Gisella gestured vehemently, her face vivid with determination. 'Now, I may find out that there's a perfectly good reason why they have to leave the cottage, but in that case they should be told what it is, not bullied out of the way. If your distrust of journalists is so great that you can't bring yourself to give me one simple piece of information, that's fine. I'll find out anyway. It'll just take me a little longer.'

'And you won't let anything stand in your way? You're a real journalist, aren't you?' Coming from Strachan, it was clearly not a compliment.

Gisella met his eyes defiantly. 'I'm just doing what I can to help. It seems to me that you can help more effectively by doing something practical than by standing around wringing your hands and exclaiming how terrible it all is. If that makes me unpopular, so be it. I'm not going to give up on the Donalds just because I'm afraid you'll think I'm an objectionable journalist. Better that than prejudiced and pig-headed!'

She flung the last words at Strachan, and his eyes narrowed dangerously. 'Don't push me too far, Gisella,' he warned through set teeth. 'Or one of these days you'll say something you'll regret!' Clicking his fingers for Bran, he strode over to the Land Rover, which was parked at a precarious angle on the rough verge. Strachan's expression was thunderous as he started the engine, and the vehicle moved forward, but it stopped as he came level with Gisella, who was still standing stormy-eyed outside the cottage, hugging her cardigan about her for warmth.

'I sold to a London company called Parker Judd,' he said grudgingly. 'They just wanted to invest in some land, and I heard that they sold on a few months ago.' He began to wind up his window again as Gisella opened her mouth. 'And before you ask, no, I don't know who the new owners are.' With that he let out the clutch and drove off up the lane before Gisella had a chance to thank him.

'That man!' She slammed the cottage door behind her as she went in to find Meg. 'He's impossible!'

'You didn't seem to be handling him with your usual cool control, I must say,' said Meg with a twinkle in her eye. She handed Gisella a mug of coffee. 'You didn't tell me he was *that* gorgeous!'

'I didn't tell you he was gorgeous at all, Meg!'

'Of course he is,' Meg said firmly. 'Tall, dark, blue-eyed, masterful-looking . . . what more do you want?'

'A touch of charm would be nice.' Gisella sat down at the kitchen table and scowled at the fridge. Meg pulled out a chair opposite her.

'I'll bet he's loaded with it.'

'Strachan?' Gisella snorted. 'He's about as charming as a lump of granite!'

'Rubbish! You're just not going about him the right way. He needs to see you as a woman, not just as a pushy journalist. Now, Ellen says he's definitely going to be at the party on Saturday, and she'd be delighted for you to come too, so it's an ideal opportunity for you to knock him sideways!'

'Hmm.' Gisella stared morosely down into her mug. 'I could try, but he hasn't been very impressed by me so far, to say the least. I get the feeling he's not the susceptible type.'

'All the better,' said Meg cheerfully. 'It'll do you good to have a bit of a challenge. Your trouble is that you're too used to men dropping at your feet as soon as you smile. This time you're just going to have to make a bit more of an effort.'

Gisella gave a reluctant grin. She was too used to her looks to be vain, but perhaps Meg was right. Perhaps she *should* make more of an effort to charm her way past Strachan's formidable defences. It would certainly be a challenge to captivate a man so determined to dislike her, and her eyes shone clear and grey with a kind of exhilaration at the thought.

'I'll have a go,' she said to Meg. 'I'm not getting very far trying to reason with him, so I've nothing to lose.' She had made up her mind, and somehow getting the article written faded into insignificance beside the importance of making Strachan regret that he had been so disagreeable. The next time Strachan met her, she vowed, he would see her as all woman!

CHAPTER SIX

BY THE following morning, the swelling on Gisella's ankle had subsided, but she ordered a taxi to take her into Crieston rather than risk driving. She wanted to rest her ankle as much as possible, as she was determined not to be limping when she saw Strachan again on Saturday. It would only remind him of their previous meetings, and she wanted to make a fresh start if she was to have any chance of attracting him.

Finding the owner of Mrs Donald's cottage proved to be a little more difficult than Gisella had anticipated, even though she had a head start with the name Strachan had given her. Someone, she thought, had been careful to cover their tracks by using the name of subsidiary companies, but their plans were clear enough. They had applied for permission to build a luxurious health and beauty centre, and the Donalds' cottage stood fair and square in the middle of the site. The planning application said that the cottage was empty, and Gisella's lips tightened. They were so sure they would get the Donalds out without any trouble!

It took some time, but eventually she established that the cottage was now owned outright by a company called CWR Holdings, whose chairman was listed as William Ross. The name meant nothing to Gisella, and she came out of the council offices in a thoughtful mood. It was time she paid a visit to the local paper.

The *Crieston Echo* occupied a rather shabby building just off the high street. Gisella paused outside to inspect the photographs in the window. Most were of local weddings—brides in white froth with fresh-faced grooms smiling grimly at the camera—but there was also a display plugging the amateur dramatics group—about to perform *The Importance Of Being Earnest*, Gisella noted. Pride of place was given to a recent visit to Crieston by a duchess, who was flanked by two prize-winning bulls.

Gisella smiled, and pushed open the door. The editor seemed delighted to meet her when she introduced herself and, even better, was an admirer of her old paper. His name was Iain Douglas, he told her, and he had been greatly impressed by her investigative pieces. He was a big, sandy man and Gisella warmed to him immediately. It made a nice change to meet someone who wasn't ridiculously prejudiced against reporters, she thought, thinking how different Iain's welcome was to Strachan McLeod's.

Strachan hadn't bothered to hide his dislike of her profession, and he seemed impervious to her looks. Gisella had never met anyone who was quite so unresponsive to her charms, and her confidence had taken a greater knock than she was prepared to admit. Iain's obvious admiration was balm to her sore feelings, and she accepted with alacrity when he suggested that they go and have some lunch, correctly interpreting this to mean a liquid one.

She was perfectly happy when Iain suggested that they take his chief reporter, Alan Wates, with them, but she soon regretted it. Alan had yet to make the big break into the national papers, and he was clearly jealous of her early success. It didn't help when Iain turned to him after Gisella had told him that she was following up the Donalds' plight, and asked why he hadn't come up with any similar stories. Gisella's heart sank when she saw Alan glare at her. She had enough problems with Strachan's disliking her without having to fight against Alan's resentment too. There must be something in the Scottish air that made her so unpopular!

'Does the name William Ross mean anything to you?' she asked hastily.

'Sure.' Iain raised one sandy eyebrow and sent Alan off to the bar for another round of drinks. 'Bill Ross is a well-known figure round here. Town councillor, successful businessman, local do-gooder...you know the type. Why are you interested in him?'

Gisella told him about the Donalds and what she had discovered that morning. 'William Ross seems to have gone to some trouble not to have his name on any of the records of ownership,' she finished.

Iain whistled. 'Bill Ross? Are you sure? He's got a squeaky-clean reputation round here. I've never cared for the man myself, but there's no doubt he does a lot for the community.'

'That's not much comfort to the Donalds, is it?' Gisella pointed out. 'If I can find out why Mr Clean is intent on evicting an elderly couple from their home, can I do a story on it for you?'

The editor's eyes narrowed. 'You'd have to be able to prove it.'

'Naturally.' She paused. Editors were notoriously tight-fisted when it came to commissioning articles. 'You wouldn't have to pay me,' she said. 'I'll do the story for free.'

That clinched it. 'All right,' said Iain. 'But you'll have to produce a watertight case against Ross before I'll publish, mind. I don't want to end up in a libel case!'

Gisella sat back with a grin. 'Thanks, Iain. You won't regret it.'

Alan came back from the bar just then, and the conversation turned to more general topics. Delighted at having persuaded Iain to let her do the story, Gisella sipped her gin and tonic and looked around her for the first time. It seemed to be a popular meeting place, and she commented on how busy it was.

'Is it always like this?'

'It's Thursday,' said Alan, as if the answer were obvious and, seeing Gisella look mystified, Iain hastened to explain.

'Thursday's market day in Crieston, so all the farmers are in town. The market is just round the corner from here, so they all come in for a drink afterwards to grumble about the prices.'

Gisella hardly heard him. She was looking at the farmer who had just come into the bar.

It was Strachan McLeod, and he had a girl with him.

Gisella's grey eyes narrowed. The girl was slight and pretty, with a rosy, doll-like complexion and a dark, shiny cap of hair. She looked neat and wholesome, and Gisella disliked her on sight.

Strachan hadn't noticed her. He took the girl by the arm and guided her over to a quiet table by the window. He seemed to know many of the people in the room, for he stopped to exchange a word with several on the way, and nodded in a friendly way at others. In spite of being dressed like all the other farmers, he had a distinctive presence that set him apart.

Gisella watched him smiling as he greeted a gnarled old farmer who had a lugubrious expression. He had never smiled at her with that unshadowed warmth, she thought with more than a touch of pique. She couldn't decide whether she wanted Strachan to notice her or not. It was infuriating to be so aware of him when he didn't even know that she was in the room!

'That's Strachan McLeod,' Iain said, turning to follow her gaze. 'The McLeods used to be big landowners round here, but Strachan had to sell off a lot of the land.' He shook his head. 'Things can't have been easy for him.'

'He can't complain,' Alan said in a hard voice. He lit a cigarette and blew out the smoke contemptuously. 'Life can't be that tough when you live in a castle!'

Gisella thought of the crumbling walls, the penetrating cold and the rain leaking into the bedrooms. Effectively, Strachan probably lived in fewer rooms than Alan did, but she didn't say so.

'Why did he have to sell off so much land?' she asked instead.

'The estate went bankrupt, I believe,' Iain told her. 'There was some kind of scandal, but it was long before I came to Crieston, so I don't know much about it. Frankly, I'm surprised McLeod's managed to keep going at all. It's hard enough making a living as a farmer as it is, without having to pay death duties and keep up a great ruin of a castle at the same time!'

'Who's that with him?' Gisella couldn't resist asking.

Iain glanced over his shoulder again. 'I think that's Elspeth Drummond. He could probably solve some of his money headaches by marrying *her*. The Drummonds are rolling in it!'

'Really?' Gisella said coldly, wishing that she hadn't asked. Her lips tightened as she watched Elspeth laugh prettily up at Strachan. For someone supposedly so averse to women, he didn't seem to have any problems coping with the fact that she kept leaning towards him and putting her hand on his arm! True, he didn't look all that enthusiastic, but compared to the dour expression he used whenever he looked at Gisella he was positively jolly. Perhaps he was thinking about all that Drummond money?

Iain and Alan were deeply involved in a discussion about the economy and, although Gisella tried hard to show an interest, her eyes kept sliding back to that table by the window.

Her smoky gaze would rest on the strong lines of Strachan's features as he listened to Elspeth—

Elspeth! How Scottish could you get?—and then she would remember and wrench her eyes away, back to Iain, or her gin, or the ashtray on the table, anything other than the angles of his face and the shape of his mouth.

'What do you think, Gisella?'

Gisella had no idea what they had been talking about. 'I agree with you, Iain,' she said firmly. 'Absolutely.'

It earned her another black look from Alan, but she didn't even notice. Her eyes had skittered back to Strachan. He was looking reflectively down into his beer, and nodding at something Elspeth was saying. What if she was suggesting a date for the wedding? Gisella thought with a quite illogical burst of panic. She wanted to scream at him to think about what he was doing, to shake his head, to stop agreeing like that.

Just then, Strachan looked up, so abruptly that Gisella wondered for a moment whether she had shouted out loud after all. His sharp blue gaze swung around the bar, glanced over Gisella and passed on for an instant before jerking back in a classic double take.

It was too late for her to look away. As the blue eyes stared into hers, Gisella felt as if she had dived into an icy pool and was fighting to catch her breath. The two of them might have been alone in the crowded bar. She couldn't read the expression in his eyes. She only knew that they held her immobile while her senses leapt and her pulse surged wildly out of control.

She wanted to smile a cool smile and turn casually away. Hadn't she vowed to make him aware of her as a woman? Why couldn't she simply curve her lips and let her eyelashes sweep her cheeks invitingly? She had done it a thousand times before. She couldn't understand why she was sitting here gawkily like this, just *staring* at him . . .

Gisella never knew how long she sat there, pinned by that blue, blue look. It might have been a matter of seconds, it might have been hours, before his gaze shifted suddenly to take in her companions. A faint expression of contempt crossed his face, and then he turned very deliberately back to Elspeth with a smile.

Gradually, Gisella became aware of the hubbub of the bar over the boom of her pulse. Iain and Alan had taken the short step from economy to politics, and had noticed nothing amiss. Her hand shook as she picked up her gin and took an uncertain sip as she tried to pull herself together.

What on earth was the matter with her? She felt unsettled, on edge, torn between a sick, fluttery excitement and a dull sense of misery simply because Strachan was smiling at another girl.

Gisella put her glass down with a click, as pride came to her rescue. If Strachan McLeod preferred a suitable, sensible Scottish girl, it was his loss!

Determined to show him the dazzling company he was missing, Gisella turned to Iain and Alan and skilfully drew their attention back to her. She positively scintillated, flirting outrageously with both of them, and telling wickedly funny stories until Iain held his sides and even Alan had to laugh.

Out of the corner of her eye, Gisella watched Strachan. Iain's guffaws had attracted everyone's attention, she saw. Everyone except Strachan, that was. He was studiously ignoring the hilarity, but a muscle worked in his jaw. Gisella was satisfied. She winked at a lad sitting at the table next to Strachan and he coloured with pleasure at being noticed by the vibrantly glamorous girl who was keeping everyone so entertained on the other side of the room.

Deciding that she had made her point, Gisella stood up to go. She said goodbye to Iain and Alan, promising to be in touch soon, and walked out of the bar. Her ankle was tender, but she gritted her teeth and made it outside without limping. It was worth it to make a stylish exit and know that every pair of eyes, with one notable exception, was watching her. Strachan might not want to acknowledge her, but at least he would have to listen to everyone else talking about her!

She wasn't going to push her luck, though. It was enough that she had made him realise that she wasn't quite the idiot he thought she was. He would have seen that other men, at least, found her attractive and amusing, but the next time they met she was going to surprise him by being different again. She was going to be quiet and serious and utterly charming. Gisella's eyes were alight with unspoken challenge. He wouldn't be able to resist her!

She dressed for the party with care. Strachan would hate anything too loud, which was a shame as she had brought some really eye-stopping outfits with her, but in the end she chose a classic little black dress. It was simply, even austerely cut, but the lack of frills ought to appeal to him, surely?

She turned slowly in front of the mirror, inspecting her reflection critically. It was demurely styled at the neck, but allowed a generous length of leg as compensation, which somehow merely served to emphasise her deceptively fragile slenderness. Although the dress was an unrelieved black, she knew that the warm texture of the material threw the glow of her skin into flattering relief and provided a dramatic foil to the smoky eyes and the ash-gold of her hair.

The utter simplicity of the dress meant that she could get away with vivid colours in her make-up. Gisella had a deep fuchsia-pink lipstick which looked wonderful, but she put it aside reluctantly, remembering Strachan's caustic comments. 'Discreet' was her motto tonight, she reminded herself, as she applied the merest hint of blusher.

Unfortunately, one glance around the room as she arrived was enough to realise that the black dress looked impossibly sophisticated in comparison to what everyone else was wearing. Gisella suppressed a sigh, seeing that all her efforts to look subtle and conventional had been utterly wasted. She might as well have gone the whole hog and worn the fuchsia lipstick after all!

She noticed Strachan as soon as she walked in, but pretended that she hadn't. This time, she was prepared for the lurch of her senses when she saw him, and was determined to stay cool. Nobody watching her greet her hostess would have guessed that her awareness was straining towards the tall, dark man standing by the fireplace.

She had never seen him in a tie before. He was wearing a beautifully cut tweed jacket over a plain white shirt and dark trousers. The unpretentious formality suited his austere features, thought Gisella. Some men had blurry outlines, but not Strachan. He had a quiet but unmistakable presence. Everything about him was well-defined somehow, so that he stood out in the crowd.

Not that she gave any sign that she had even recognised him! Mindful of her new, sober image, Gisella began to circulate. She kept her voice low, and made no effort to attract any attention to herself, choosing, rather, to talk quietly with some of the more elderly guests, who found her charmingly interested in their lives, and refreshingly modest about her own career. They hardly noticed how she brought the conversation round to Kilnacroish, but she didn't learn much. They were united in liking and admiring Strachan, but would only shake their heads and say that it was very sad when she tried to steer them towards the past.

Meg's husband, Neil, kept a wary eye on her. They had picked Gisella up earlier that evening, and he had spent the entire trip impressing upon her the need to not embarrass him by pestering Strachan McLeod. 'Please remember that we have to live here,' he said austerely. He had heard all about Gisella's—in his view—ill-judged attempts to gain access to Castle Kilnacroish. 'McLeod is a respected member of the community, and I don't want to be associated with any plan you're hatching up.' He distrusted Gisella when she was quiet and well-behaved even more than when she was the centre of attention! Sometimes he thought she had no regard for convention at all.

'Stop looking so worried!' Gisella hissed in his ear as she passed him on her way to the dining-room for the buffet supper. 'I'm not going to explode!'

'I just don't trust you,' he muttered back.

'If you don't stop looking suspicious of me, I'm going to tell everyone that we're having an affair,' Gisella threatened mischievously.

'You wouldn't!'

Neil looked so aghast that Gisella couldn't help laughing. Unfortunately, it rather spoilt her quiet image, and she stopped as soon as she saw that people were turning their heads to see who had that loud, delightfully infectious laugh.

Turning quickly away, she literally bumped into Strachan McLeod. Her senses flared into awareness at the brief touch of their bodies, so that even if she hadn't been able to see she would have known immediately who it was. Stay cool, she reminded herself fiercely as she stepped back.

'I'm so sorry——' She broke off with a well-feigned start of surprise. 'Why, hello! Fancy seeing you here!'

'Our paths do seem doomed to cross,' Strachan said in his dourest voice. 'Are you the entertainer for tonight?'

'Entertainer?'

'I thought Ellen might have booked you to keep everyone amused,' he explained, his dark blue eyes cold and unfriendly. 'You gave such a good performance in the bar the other day that I imagine your fame must have spread. You've been pretty quiet so far, but when I heard you laugh just now I had a sinking feeling that you were warming up for another exhibition!'

'I didn't realise that having a good time wasn't allowed at parties in Scotland,' Gisella snapped back, immediately provoked into forgetting her meek and mild image. 'It must have spoilt your lunch on Thursday to see people actually enjoying themselves! And laughing! Heaven forbid!'

Strachan ignored her sarcasm. 'Seeing three journalists with their heads together was enough to spoil my lunch,' he said bitingly. 'Whose reputation were you planning to tear to shreds? Iain Douglas and his sidekick don't usually get up to much harm, but I wouldn't put it past you to encourage them to start digging up some dirt.'

'If the dirt's there, don't you think it *should* be dug up?' Gisella retorted, thinking about William Ross and his plans to evict the Donalds. 'You can cover dirt up and pretend it's not there, but it doesn't go away. It just gets dirtier.'

'Very eloquent!' he sneered. 'I'd be a little more impressed if you concentrated on the real dirt instead of inventing it whenever it suits you!'

Gisella was keeping a tight rein on her temper. 'I have *never* invented anything. Believe me, there's quite enough real dirt, as you call it, without having to make anything up. There simply isn't any point in being anything less than honest.'

'That's rich coming from a girl who's been going round telling people that she's a frustrated novelist!' Strachan retorted. 'It's not quite the same thing as being a hard-nosed journalist, is it?'

'I *am* a frustrated novelist,' said Gisella, losing patience. 'And I wouldn't be frustrated if I could just finish my article about the Candle Tower!'

'Oh, dear, oh, dear!' he mocked. 'So I'm the reason you're so frustrated, am I, Gisella?'

Gisella's grey eyes met his blue ones resentfully. She had blown it already! What was it about him that made her lose her cool? He only had to look at her and all her careful plans disintegrated into frustrated anger and a disconcerting awareness of him. 'I'll finish the article somehow,' she said between clenched teeth.

'Not if I can help it,' he promised. 'You may have managed to persuade everyone here that you're sweet and charming, Gisella, but I know better. I've come across journalists before, and it'll take more than a pair of big grey eyes and a bewitching smile to make me trust one!'

They glared at each other, antagonism crackling in the air between them. How had she thought she could ever charm him? Gisella wondered crossly. How had she thought she *wanted* to? He was insufferable.

'Strachan?' Elspeth Drummond appeared suddenly by his side and touched his arm with a winsome smile. 'Are you coming to have some supper?' Her brown eyes were cold as she glanced at Gisella, and it was obvious that she had come to rescue Strachan from her clutches.

With some reluctance, Strachan introduced them, and the two girls tried to look pleased to meet each other. Each knew perfectly well who the other was.

'Have you come to stay in the area, or are you just visiting?' Elspeth asked sweetly, evidently hoping that Gisella would say that she was just passing through.

'I *was* just going to stay a few months, but everyone's been so kind and friendly that I'm tempted to move up here permanently,' Gisella lied, equally sweetly, knowing that they would be horrified at the idea of having her on their doorstep forever.

'I'm so glad you like it here,' Elspeth said insincerely. 'But I can't help feeling you might get a little bored after a while. We're very countrified up here, aren't we?' Her glance up at Strachan was designed to show Gisella exactly who he belonged with. 'I think you might find us all rather unsophisticated for you.'

In other words, you'll never belong. Gisella was no fool. Elspeth was telling her to keep off her territory. 'I'm sure I won't get bored,' she said with a smile. 'I'm interested in everything, and the longer I stay, the more I find to interest me round here.'

It was a subtle threat, and not missed by Strachan. There was a gleam in his blue eyes, but it was impossible to tell whether it was exasperation or reluctant amusement.

'As for being too sophisticated,' Gisella went on, 'my friends will be able to tell you that I'm a very simple girl at heart!'

'Simply infuriating?' Strachan suggested in a murmur, and Gisella sent him a daggered look as she dragged Neil ruthlessly forward. 'This is Neil Fraser,' she said. She might as well prove that she did have friends. 'We're old friends, aren't we, Neil?'

Neil looked appalled at the thought of being labelled a friend of hers. 'Gisella is really a friend of my wife's,' he excused himself to Strachan.

That was definitely amusement in Strachan's eyes now as he watched Gisella glare at Neil's poor-spirited support. 'I think I've heard of you,' he said pleasantly to Neil. 'Aren't you a solicitor?'

Neil nodded, clearly gratified at having been pointed out to such a respected local figure, but his smile vanished as Strachan went on.

'You're just the person to give me some advice about how to deal with trespassers. I've been having quite a problem recently with people wandering on to my land. It's getting to be a nuisance.'

'Have you?' Elspeth sounded surprised and Gisella took some comfort from the fact that Strachan hadn't told her about the disastrous escapade. They couldn't be that close.

She got in quickly before Neil had a chance to reply. 'It's funny you should say that,' she said with a bright smile. 'I was talking to someone the other day, and they told me that there isn't in fact a law against trespass in Scotland.' It had come up in conversation with Iain Douglas, and she had filed the information away in her mind as a matter of habit. 'That's right, isn't it, Neil?' she asked, turning to him with a warning glint in her eye.

'Strictly speaking——' Neil was looking agonised, clearly convinced that Gisella was bent on embarrassing him in front of these local dignitaries.

'So landowners can't go around threatening people left, right and centre if they happen to lose their way,' Gisella swept on before he had a chance to go any further. 'I never knew that before, did you?' She tilted her chin at Strachan, her eyes bright with unspoken challenge.

'I'm sure there's a law against invasion of one's privacy,' Strachan retorted. 'It comes to the same thing, after all.'

'Every Scotsman's home is his castle, you mean?' Gisella misquoted with something of a snap. 'Especially yours!'

'Exactly,' he said.

The atmosphere between them was alive with an electric awareness. Elspeth frowned, not pleased to see Strachan's attention fixed on the alarmingly attractive English girl, even if he did look more hostile than charmed.

'We'd better go and get some supper,' she said to Strachan, pointedly excluding Gisella and Neil. She took his arm and tugged at it possessively.

Neil was equally anxious to get Gisella away from Strachan. He could feel her simmering with defiance beside him in the uncomfortably explosive atmosphere. There was no telling what she would do when she was like this.

'Let me introduce you to the Bairds,' he said, taking Gisella's elbow firmly and urging her away.

Involuntarily, Gisella and Strachan glanced at each other, both being determinedly pulled apart like scrapping dogs. The absurdity of the situation lit their eyes with laughter at the same time, and for a brief, unthinking moment they grinned, acknowledging the unexpectedly shared tug of humour. They had laughed together once before, and Gisella felt the same sharp jab of recognition.

The next instant it had vanished, as if they were both scared at having revealed too much. Gisella tilted her chin and Strachan's eyes shuttered, and they turned away at the same time, both glad to have remembered their animosity before it was too late.

CHAPTER SEVEN

GISELLA was still in fighting mood when Meg and Neil dropped her at the cottage later that night. Strachan's total lack of susceptibility to her charms rankled. All that effort dressing discreetly to impress him completely wasted! He hadn't been in the slightest bit captivated. True, she hadn't helped by losing her temper but, still, he could have shown *some* interest... Instead, she was the one left feeling ruffled and she didn't like it at all! Now she was utterly determined to get into Castle Kilnacroish, just to prove to Strachan McLeod that she wouldn't let him get the better of her that easily!

In spite of the unsuccessful encounter with Strachan, the party had given Gisella much food for thought. She was curious about the mystery surrounding Strachan's financial straits and why it had given him such an abiding distrust of journalists. All her efforts to probe the past at the party had been in vain; she had never met such a discreet group of people. Local people were her most obvious source of information, but since they were all being so reticent she would have to try elsewhere.

The next morning she rang the librarian on her old paper. He was an old friend, and when they had exchanged news she asked him to see if he could find any newspaper cuttings about Kilnacroish. 'I haven't got much information to go on, I'm afraid,' she said. 'It might not even have been a big story, but if there was anything in the papers it would have been about ten years ago, maybe more.'

If there had been even a tiny snippet, she knew that Jeff would find it. The library held cuttings from all the major papers, carefully filed by subjects and cross-referenced to names where necessary, and Jeff had an uncanny ability to produce information on the most obscure of subjects. He promised to post her what he could find, and Gisella thanked him profusely before she rang off.

She sat with her hand on the phone, plotting her next move. Meg had introduced her to an imposing woman called Mrs McInnes, whom Gisella had no difficulty in identifying as the local busybody. By her own account, Mrs McInnes was involved with everything and knew everybody, and Gisella had listened intently when she had described the musical evening and reception she was planning in aid of one of the local charities. Thanks to 'dear Strachan', it was being held in the big hall at Castle Kilnacroish.

'People do so love a historic setting,' Mrs McInnes confided. 'Castle Kilnacroish is always very popular. It has such an atmosphere.'

Privately, Gisella thought that central heating would be more of an asset in November, but she kept her reflections to herself. Charmed by her interest, Mrs McInnes found herself led on to talk about the reception, and even the problems the committee was having in finding waitresses for it. 'Girls nowadays think you should pay them the earth to go out on a cold night. You'd think they'd be glad of the work!'

Gisella broke in before Mrs McInnes had a chance to hold forth on her views about what was wrong with the younger generation. 'I think I might know of someone who'd like the occasional evening job,' she said, improvising quickly. 'Why don't you give me the number, and I'll suggest she gives you a ring?'

It was too good an opportunity to miss. Gisella looked down at the number in her hand. Delighted, Mrs McInnes had told her that a Mrs Forbes was the person to contact. 'Do encourage your friend to ring her,' she had said. 'We're desperately short of staff, and the reception's next week. I don't know what we shall do if we can't find some more people.'

Gisella lifted the receiver. She had always been a good mimic, and it never occurred to Mrs Forbes that Mary Cameron was not exactly who she said she was: a nice girl from Kirkcaldy who was having trouble making ends meet. She was too pleased at having found another waitress to ask many questions, and Gisella was relieved to find an interview would not be necessary.

'Just turn up at the castle next Wednesday at six o'clock, and ask for me,' said Mrs Forbes. 'Wear a black dress if you can, and we'll provide you with an apron when you get here.'

Gisella wondered what the reaction would be if she arrived in the little black dress she had worn to the party, but reluctantly decided that her disguise demanded something a little less sophisticated. On her next visit to Crieston, she bought herself a suitably dull dress which had nothing to recommend it other than the fact that it was undeniably black.

She giggled as she studied her reflection on Wednesday evening. She had never worn anything quite so dowdy, and by the time she had put on a wig of brown curls, and Neil's spare pair of glasses, which she had wheedled out of Meg, she was unrecognisable.

Gisella was confident that she could get away with it. Nobody ever looked at the waitresses unless they had some disaster, and it couldn't be *that* difficult to hand round a few glasses of wine at the interval. When they had all gone back to the concert, there was bound to be an opportunity to slip away for a few minutes.

No, it couldn't go wrong. Gisella tucked the plan of the castle into her pocket and put on a pair of boots. There was no point in disguising herself and then driving up in a red sports car, after all. This time she was going to have to walk.

It was all too easy, she thought later, as she waited in her apron for the first half of the concert to finish. A platform had been set up in the hall for the quartet, and the audience were no doubt freezing to death on their folding chairs but, to Gisella's relief, the reception was to be held in the drawing-room, where logs blazed in an enormous fireplace.

Gisella studied the room with interest, mentally refurnishing it. It could be so lovely! The oak panelling gave it an air of warmth which the hall so conspicuously lacked, and with the heavy brocade curtains closed against the dark night and the glow of firelight it was easy not to notice that the carpet was threadbare and the plaster ceiling crumbling.

The walls were hung with portraits in heavy gilt frames. The McLeods of Kilnacroish had been a grim lot, Gisella decided, and it was easy to see where Strachan had inherited his dour looks from. The painted eyes stared down at her in a familiar, disapproving way, and Gisella poked out her tongue at them before turning ostentatiously away to study the patch over the fireplace where another picture had once hung.

'That was a Rembrandt,' Mrs Forbes said, appearing beside Gisella and following her gaze. 'Such a shame that the collection had to go! But Strachan has done a marvellous job, considering.'

Considering *what*? Gisella wanted to ask in frustration, but at the moment there was a burst of applause from the hall.

'Here they come now.' Mrs Forbes hurried off and Gisella hastily put on Neil's glasses as the audience began to drift into the drawing-room in search of refreshment. The glasses distorted her vision horribly, and she had to squint in one eye just to see where she was going.

She had been given two trays of nibbles to hand around, and she kept her eyes carefully lowered as if she were shy. There was a surprising number of people there but, as she had expected, none of them bothered to look beyond the food. Peering through Neil's glasses, Gisella recognised quite a few people from Ellen's party, even if they did look rather blurred. She could see Mrs McInnes on the other side of the room, and resolved to avoid her at all costs. The old girl had sharp eyes, and wouldn't miss much.

There was no sign of Strachan, but Elspeth was there, looking fresh-faced and pretty in a red dress. She was talking to a florid man whom Gisella recognised from the photographs she had seen: William Ross.

Gisella watched him coolly. Over the past few days she had managed to find out a good deal about Ross's activities, certainly a lot more than he would want her to know. Ross might be playing the good citizen tonight, but Gisella knew better. The Donalds were not the only people who had come up against his ruthless business sense. Only yesterday she had talked to a couple with two young children who had found themselves suddenly homeless, and tomorrow she would be meeting one of his ex-employees who she hoped might be able to tell her more about Ross's secretive business methods.

A startled murmur by the door jerked Gisella's attention away from William Ross. For those who had never seen him before, Bran's enormous size was undoubtedly a shock, but she had eyes only for the man at whose side he stood.

Strachan was every inch the laird tonight. He wore the kilt with a magnificent sporran, and the silver buttons on his short, dark jacket gleamed. A dirk was strapped to his calf over the thick stockings. At ease in the traditional costume, he none the less looked tough and uncompromising and Gisella's heart began to beat a little faster. He didn't look like a man to cross.

He was standing with the musicians, while Mrs Forbes hovered around, pressing glasses of wine into their hands. Gisella began to back away, but Mrs Forbes was too quick for her. Glancing round for a waitress, she caught Gisella's eye and beckoned her over. 'Mary!'

Reluctantly, Gisella slunk over, keeping her eyes humbly lowered as she offered the trays round. 'Have a sausage roll,' she muttered. All she could see of Strachan was his hand as he took one. It looked strong and brown and infinitely competent and, with a shiver, she remembered how it had felt against her foot.

'Thank you...Mary? It was Mary, wasn't it?' Trust him to notice her! Everyone else had been quite happy just to take something and carry on with their conversation, she thought with a twinge of exasperation.

She nodded and began to back away, but Strachan seemed determined to be pleasant. 'It was good of you to come and work on such a cold night.'

'It's for a good cause,' she muttered in her Kirkcaldy accent.

'Have you had to come far?'

'No, not really.' Why didn't he shut up and go back to his companions?

'Where are you from?'

Gisella suppressed a sigh. 'Kirkcaldy,' she whispered, as if she were shy. She couldn't look at him directly; she was sure he would recognise her.

'Kirkcaldy?' She could swear he was enjoying himself. 'You're a long way from home. What are you doing over here?'

For a terrible moment Gisella's mind went blank. She stared down at her sausage rolls in panic. What *would* she be doing? 'My boyfriend's from these parts,' she improvised wildly.

She could have kissed the musician who recalled Strachan's attention just then, before he had a chance to ask her any more embarrassing questions. It was typically obstructive of him to turn chatty just when she least wanted it.

'She's a nice girl, but awfully shy,' Gisella could hear Mrs Forbes whispering as she edged away, relieved that he hadn't seen through her disguise.

She had reckoned without Bran as she slipped through the crowd, and it was only when she began to notice the curious glances and smiles that she thought to look over her shoulder. Bran was following her, his tail wagging and his dark eyes hopeful as he waited for her to notice him.

Gisella's heart sank, but she carried on grimly offering round the trays as if the enormous dog at her heels had nothing whatsoever to do with her. Bran couldn't have found a surer way of attracting attention to her if he had tried! People kept commenting on him and asking her if she knew she had a friend following her. As if she wouldn't be aware of an animal that size dogging her footsteps!

'I think he's just after the sausage rolls,' she explained with a smile, mentally cursing Bran.

'Go away!' she whispered at him as she reloaded the plates from the table, but he merely nudged her affectionately with his cold black nose.

Gisella didn't dare look round to see if Strachan had noticed his dog's strange behaviour. She picked up the plates again and prepared to do another round. Bran showed every intention of following her. 'Go and adore someone else!' she said between her teeth and tried to nudge him away from her. That was the wrong thing to do, because Bran immediately thought she was playing a game and barked with excitement.

'Oh, well done!' Gisella muttered to him sarcastically, as the entire room stopped talking to turn and look at them. Trying to look baffled by the dog's attention, she plunged back into the crowd before Strachan got a good look at her.

'Here, Bran! Here, boy!' Out of the corner of her eye, she could see Elspeth clicking her fingers at the dog as she told everyone how good she was with animals. 'I love dogs,' she was saying. 'They're such good judges of character, don't you think? They don't care if you're not clever or sophisticated. You can never fool a dog, no matter how hard you try, and Bran's cleverer than most, aren't you, boy?'

Gisella managed to carry on watching Elspeth as she handed round the plates. She was obviously trying to impress everyone with the fact that she knew Strachan's dog so well. Gisella was delighted to see that Bran refused to respond to her call, so Elspeth was forced to come over and take hold of his collar while she petted him.

'Are you worrying about next weekend?' she asked him in a high, silly voice. 'Don't worry, I'll bring Strachan back to you!' she said, mentioning oh, so casually to the group around her that she and Strachan would be going away together. 'He's a bit big for us to take along, so he's going to stay and guard the castle,' she explained prettily.

Gisella eyed her with acute dislike. She obviously liked to give the impression that she and Strachan were an established couple, but anyone could see that Bran wasn't too keen on the idea. His manners were too good to allow him to pull away, and he stood and suffered her pats, but with such an air of martyrdom that Gisella had to quickly suppress a grin.

She took the opportunity to slip out of his sight. Mrs McInnes was chivvying everyone to go back to the hall for the second half, and they began to drift slowly away, reluctant to leave the warmth of the fire. Over by the door, Strachan snapped his fingers for Bran, who immediately broke away from Elspeth and loped over to his side. Elspeth looked a little put out, but put a brave face on it, following the dog and standing next to Strachan so that they looked like a couple.

Gisella turned her back so that they couldn't see her face and busied herself tidying up glasses. Now that the rush was over, the other waitresses relaxed and chatted together, and it wasn't difficult to slip away without their noticing.

A small ante-room led off from the drawing-room, and Gisella paused in there to take off Neil's wretched glasses and orientate herself from her plan of the castle layout. If the plan was right, the stone staircase in here should lead up to the gallery, and at the far end she should find the stairway to the tower.

The quartet were keeping everyone occupied in the hall, the waitresses were resting their feet; there would never be a better time. Taking a deep breath, Gisella crept up the stairs and along the gallery which ran over part of the hall. The music floated clearly up the grand staircase and there was enough light to see by, although Gisella kept to the deep shadows along the far wall.

The stairway was hidden behind a studded oak door, and Gisella's heart beat faster as she reached for the handle. The next moment it almost stopped as a voice made her swing round with a gasp of terror.

'Don't you ever give up?' asked Strachan, exasperated.

Gisella collapsed back against the door with a hand at her throat. Her heart was beating so frantically that she could hardly speak.

'You frightened me,' she gasped.

'I thought I'd made my views on your poking around my castle very plain?'

'I don't know what you mean,' Gisella muttered, quickly resuming her Mary Cameron voice. 'I'm just checking to see if there are any glasses up here——'

'You needn't bother with that silly accent, Gisella. I know perfectly well who you are.'

She gave up. 'How did you guess?'

'I'd know you anywhere,' he sighed. 'Even in that ridiculous wig and carrying a tray of sausage rolls, your style is unmistakable!'

'I bet I'd have got away with it if it hadn't been for Bran,' she grumbled. 'Dogs ought to be kept in kennels, not allowed to hound waitresses. I felt ridiculous with him trailing after me like that!'

'If you dress up in a laughable disguise like the one you've got on, you should be prepared to feel ridiculous,' Strachan said unsympathetically. 'I must admit that I never thought I'd see you looking so frumpy,' he went on, eyeing her derisively. 'You must be desperate to get into the tower if you're prepared to wear a dress like that! It really does nothing for you.'

Gisella clenched her fists. 'I thought you liked the dowdy look?'

'Not on you.' Strachan reached out and pulled the wig off her head so that the blonde hair tumbled about her face, catching the light from the stairwell. 'Why are you so stubborn?' he asked irritably, but there was a strange undercurrent in his voice. 'You've been like a thorn in my side ever since you arrived up here with your golden hair and your grey eyes.'

Dropping the wig to the floor, he twisted his fingers in the softness of her hair almost thoughtfully. 'You're everything I distrust in a woman, Gisella,' he said in a low voice. 'I keep wishing you'd go away and stop pestering me, but somehow you've got under my skin. I think about the way you laugh and the way you lift your chin when you're cross, and sometimes I can even forget you're a journalist. Not for long though.'

He was standing very close, and Gisella's heart, which had been pounding so frantically, slowed right down until she could hardly breathe. She was mesmerised by his nearness, by the fingers entwined in her hair. Her eyes were fixed on one of the silver buttons on his jacket. It gleamed through the shadows like a single point of light.

'Do you ever forget about your story, Gisella?' His voice was deep and low.

'Sometimes,' she whispered.

Strachan moved closer, and instinctively she tried to step back, only to find herself jammed against the oak door. The old iron studs dug into her back. Downstairs the quartet came to the end of a piece, and the applause echoed up the stairs.

'I'll bet you don't forget for long,' he said softly, but she could hear the bitterness and frustration in his voice. He lifted his other hand and tilted her face so that she was forced to look up at him. 'You're a journalist through and through, aren't you, Gisella?'

'Only sometimes,' she whispered again. His face was shadowed and she couldn't take her eyes from his mouth. She was almost frightened by the desire that shimmered between them, unspoken and unwanted, but unmistakable. Could he read it in her eyes? Did he know that she ached with the need to hold him close, to explore his mouth with her own, to feel his hands hard against her body?

'Damn you!' Strachan muttered, and his fingers tightened against her cheek. 'Why do you have to be the way you are?' he demanded half angrily as he bent his head and kissed her.

At the touch of his lips, the smouldering desire exploded into a blaze that ran like wildfire along Gisella's veins, making her gasp with excitement. She hadn't known that the mere touch of a mouth could be so electrifying, and her lips were warm and yielding beneath his, seeking eagerly in return.

She had forgotten her vow to get the better of him. The Candle Tower and the unfinished article faded into insignificance as the simmering cauldron of resentment and frustration and unacknowledged attraction erupted into reluctant, rocketing passion. She had forgotten everything but the touch of him and the taste of him. It was as if this was all she had wanted since he first strode across that field towards her.

As their kisses deepened, Strachan's hands moved hungrily over her body and Gisella melted into him, shuddering with delight at the hard urgency of his touch. She felt his face with her fingers, savouring the male-rough texture of his jaw as his lips left hers to burn a tantalising trail of kisses to the lobe of her ear.

'Gisella.' He buried his face against her throat, breathing in the fragrance of her skin, and murmuring her name as if in despair.

Gisella tipped back her head with a shiver of desire, and when his mouth found hers again there was a new urgency to their kisses, a wild desperation, as if they sensed that time was running out. Any minute now, reality would break in and they would have to break apart and let the old antagonism spring back between them.

Don't let it happen! Gisella thought frantically, but it was too late. Strachan was drawing away, his lips and hands lingering until the last as if they had a will of their own, but then they too were gone, leaving her to lean back against the door for support.

Strachan's breathing was ragged as he stared down at her, and she turned her head away, unable to bear the prospect of seeing the contempt creep back into his eyes. There was only the sound of their breathing, and the distant notes of the quartet.

Gisella was shaking. She ached to feel his arms about her once more, but he had taken a step back as if he no longer trusted himself near her.

'Gisella,' he began huskily, but she never knew what he was about to say, for at that moment Elspeth appeared at the top of the stairs.

She looked about her uncertainly, and then saw the two figures standing together, not touching, by the door.

'Strachan?' she said and came towards them, her high heels clicking on the wooden floor. 'Is there a problem?'

'No,' he said curtly, and swore under his breath. 'You'd better go,' he said to Gisella in the same abrupt tone, and she nodded miserably.

Then, realising that he was waiting for her to leave, she bent to retrieve the wig from the floor and walked past him without a word, head held high. She didn't even acknowledge Elspeth's presence. Later, she wondered how she had managed to put one leg in front of the other, but somehow she made it to the end of the gallery.

'What on earth is *she* doing here?' she heard Elspeth demand suspiciously. 'And why is she wearing that odd dress?'

Strachan didn't answer. His eyes were on the slender figure walking down the gallery as if in a daze.

'You'd been gone such a long time that I wondered if there was something going on,' Elspeth went on, patently waiting for an explanation, but she was to be disappointed.

'Nothing important,' he said.

Safely out of sight in the stairwell, Gisella felt her knees buckle suddenly, and she sank down on to the steps, leaning her burning cheek against the cold stone wall.

Nothing important. Is that how it seemed to Strachan?

Her senses throbbed as if he kissed her still. Hadn't he felt the same heady rush of excitement, the same desperate need, the same aching delight? Gisella closed her eyes. It was too late to deny the truth now. She was in love with Strachan, had loved him and wanted him even while she tried desperately to dislike him.

Unbidden, she remembered something Meg had once said. 'When you fall in love, it'll be with a crash—and it'll be with the last person you expect!' She had been blind not to have seen it before now.

But Strachan wasn't in love with her. The kiss had meant nothing important to him. Desolation seeped through Gisella. She had to get out of here.

Outside, it was very dark and a cold wind blew the tops of the trees about. The music from the quartet floated out into the night. Gisella turned up the collar of her coat and began trudging down the avenue, her head down against the wind.

How confident she had been when she had walked up earlier that evening! How determined not to let Strachan get the better of her! And how little it all mattered now.

Gisella had never been in love like this before, not with this aching, yearning, craving for one man's touch and one man's smile. A man who disliked her, who had told her that she was everything he despised. A man for whom she was a nuisance, a mere irritation, nothing important.

'Why do you have to be the way you are?' he had asked, and she had no answer. She only knew that that was how she was and she couldn't change. She couldn't make herself into a nice, sensible country girl, and if that was what Strachan wanted then she would go.

CHAPTER EIGHT

By the time Gisella got back to the cottage, she was deathly tired, but she knew she wouldn't sleep. Instead, she sat down and wrote the article about Isobel and the Candle Tower, pretending that she had spent the night there. She wouldn't—couldn't—pester Strachan any more.

Tomorrow she would fax her piece to Yvonne, and tie up the last loose ends on the William Ross story. Then she would be free to leave. The thought cracked her heart, even though she knew that staying would be worse. She couldn't bear to be near Strachan, knowing that she loved him, knowing that he hated her.

The print shop in Crieston had a fax machine, and she sent Yvonne her story first thing the next morning before she had a chance to change her mind. She had never written such a flat, pedestrian piece before, but at least it was done. Now there was only William Ross to sort out.

She had arranged to meet Ross's ex-employee in a seedy coffee shop at half-past ten. It was market day again, and the town was already crowded. Gisella wasted time wandering up and down the main street and pretending to look in the shop windows, but everything she saw seemed to change and shimmer into Strachan's face: strong brows, blue eyes, the unexpected sensuality of his mouth.

A dark head turning in the crowd would make her heart jolt, and every time she saw a weathered jacket or a decisive stride she would wonder, half in dread, half in longing, if she might see him after all, but it was never him.

'Hello.'

Gisella stared blankly around her, until her eyes focused and she recognised Mrs Robertson, Strachan's housekeeper.

'Oh, hello.'

'You meet everybody in Crieston on a Thursday,' Mrs Robertson said with chatty satisfaction. 'I thought I recognised you.'

Gisella was a little surprised. She had only met Mrs Robertson once, the first time she had gone to the castle, but it was obvious that the housekeeper knew exactly who she was. 'Ailsa Donald's a relative of mine,' she explained. 'She's told me how kind you've been to her. They've had a hard time what with old Archie having his accident, and now this business about the house. I don't know what they'd have done if you hadn't offered to find out what was going on.' Her shrewd brown eyes studied Gisella approvingly. 'We're all fond of Ailsa and Archie round here, so if you can help them we'd all be grateful.'

'I'll certainly do my best,' said Gisella, and then, sensing that Mrs Robertson was about to launch into voluble thanks, swiftly changed the subject. 'Are you doing your shopping?'

'Well, I thought I'd just nip in while I had the chance,' Mrs Robertson confided. 'I'm usually at the castle by now, but Mr McLeod's gone away, so I can go in a bit later.'

'Gone away?' Gisella echoed dully, and her heart tore at the thought.

'Oh, it's just for a few days.' Mrs Robertson leant closer, prepared to enjoy a good gossip. 'He's gone off with that Elspeth Drummond. She's been trying to get him away for a weekend for ages, I reckon. That one's got her sights set on being the laird's lady, you mark my words. She's always dropping by on some excuse or other, and trying to tell me what Mr McLeod would like for his tea.' She bridled with remembered indignation. 'I haven't been cooking for him for the last ten years without finding out what he likes and what he doesn't. I don't need Miss Butter-wouldn't-melt-in-my-mouth to tell me what I should be cooking!'

Clearly Mrs Robertson was not one of Elspeth's greatest fans. If Gisella had been feeling less wretched, she would have been amused, but all she could think of was that Strachan had gone away with Elspeth. She remembered now that Elspeth had been dropping hints about spending the weekend with Strachan, but she hadn't taken it seriously at the time. Now she was shocked at how much it hurt.

'Of course, he'll be back in time for the ball, don't you worry about that,' Mrs Robertson was saying.

'What ball?' Gisella forced herself to ask.

'The laird always holds a ball for the local people at Castle Kilnacroish, round about St Andrew's Day,' the housekeeper explained proudly. 'Well, we call it a ball, but it's more of a ceilidh, really. It's not grand at all. Everyone goes along and we have drinks and dancing and a few of the old songs. It makes a good break, just when you're fed up with winter and Christmas is still a way off. You must come along.'

'I might not be here,' Gisella said. Strachan wouldn't want to see her, and she couldn't bear to go along and see Elspeth acting as hostess.

'But Ailsa Donald told me you were going to live here for a few months!'

'I was, but . . .' Gisella trailed off. How could she explain to Mrs Robertson that she would have to go, to salvage what remained of her pride and pick up the threads of her old life? 'I've changed my mind,' she said lamely.

'Ah, well, I suppose you journalists always have to go where the big stories are,' Mrs Robertson said philosophically, bending to pick up her shopping basket. 'But I hope you'll stay long enough for the ball. We'd all be very glad to see you there after what you've done for the Donalds.'

At least her time here hadn't been a total disaster, Gisella thought dolefully as she drove home. Ross's ex-employee had proved a mine of useful information and, having been sacked without reason, he was more than willing to help Gisella expose the genial Ross as a fraud. She had been to the *Echo* to see Iain Douglas too, and he had promised that he would splash the story on the front page of next week's paper.

The post was lying on the mat as she let herself into the cottage, and she picked up a large envelope with a London postmark. Ripping it open, she saw that it was stuffed full of newspaper cuttings; Jeff had found more than she had expected.

Before she had a chance to look at them, the phone rang. It was Yvonne, and she was furious.

'I'm not going to thank you for this piece you faxed me, Gisella, because it was awful!' she stormed. 'I can't publish this after the lead-up we've given it! It had about as much atmosphere as a hotel brochure, and you didn't even describe the Candle Tower. That was the whole point! I don't think you've even been inside it, have you?'

'No,' said Gisella, too tired and miserable to fight back. 'No, I haven't.'

'I'm disappointed in you, Gisella!' Yvonne raged. 'You promised me that this would be the best story of all. I wouldn't have thought it would be beyond a journalist of your calibre to get into a castle. It's hardly the Kremlin, after all!'

'I've tried——'

'Well, you'll just have to try again.' Abruptly, Yvonne changed to a cajoling tone. 'You're such a good reporter, Gisella. I know you can do it. Just give it one more go. We've been plugging this series and we'll look ridiculous if we don't come up with what we've promised. Surely I don't need to remind you how many magazines have gone under in this year alone?'

'No,' Gisella sighed. 'And you don't need to remind me how hard it is to find work as a freelance, either.'

'It's not just your career that's at stake, remember,' Yvonne said, resorting to emotional blackmail. 'The editor's just looking for an excuse to get rid of people at the moment...'

Gisella's fingers tightened round the phone until her knuckles showed white. 'All right, Yvonne,' she said in a colourless voice. 'I'll rewrite the article.'

'And you'll try and spend the night in the tower?'

'I'll do what I can.' Gisella put down the receiver with a sigh. She wished she had never heard of Lady Isobel or her wretched lover. Unwilling to think about redoing the piece yet, she pulled Jeff's envelope towards her and spread the cuttings out on the table. The headlines jumped out at her.

McLeod Denies Fraud Charges
McLeod Under Investigation
Bitter Attack By McLeod's Son
McLeod In Hiding
Arrest Imminent
McLeod Mystery Death

The stories had run for months, starting from reports of rumours to full-scale investigative pieces. It was a simple enough story and, reading the cuttings, Gisella could see so clearly how it had snowballed into scandal.

Robert McLeod had been a wealthy man, with business interests far beyond the Kilnacroish estate. When his empire had started to founder, no one could tell, but as soon as the first whisper of suspicion was heard the Press were on to him. They hounded Robert McLeod, delving into his affairs with relish as his desperate measures to save his business were exposed as fraud, and the empire collapsed around him into bankruptcy. The fraud squad had been ordered in but, before any arrest could be made, Robert McLeod had been killed. His car had been found at the bottom of a steep drop. No one else had been involved and they could find nothing wrong with the brakes or steering, but in the end his death had been put down to a tragic accident.

Gisella put the last cutting slowly back on to the table. It wasn't surprising that Strachan hated journalists. Even if his father had been guilty—as it seemed he had—his hounding by the Press would be hard to forgive. Their attacks had been particularly virulent, as if they had enjoyed his fall from the comfortable life he had led between his Scottish estate and the house in Belgravia. The *Daily Examiner* had been his severest critic; now Gisella understood why Strachan had recoiled when she boasted of working for them. No wonder he had been bitter and suspicious!

She went back to the cutting about the funeral. There was a photograph of Strachan there, looking strained and somehow very young—twenty-five, it said in the article. The journalist had taken some satisfaction in explaining that he had been left with enormous debts and that the mysterious circumstances of his father's death invalidated any insurance policies. The Kilnacroish estate had been milked dry to support the bankrupt empire, and would probably have to be sold. Almost as an afterthought, he had added that Strachan's fiancée had broken off the engagement as soon as she had heard of his father's disgrace.

Gisella's eyes were dark as she thought how Strachan must have suffered. Abandoned by his father, rejected by his fiancée, crushed by debts and a devastated inheritance...how had he survived those dark days? She understood his bitterness against journalists and faithless women now. What reason had she given him to think that she was any different? She had hassled him just like all the others. Of course he despised her.

For want of anything better to do, she worked, and by Sunday evening the article on William Ross was finished. If he could see her, would Strachan think that she was hounding Ross just as others had hounded his father? Gisella was tempted to abandon the whole idea, but then she thought of the Donalds. She didn't have the right to let them down. Strachan couldn't think any worse of her than he did already and, anyway, Ross deserved to be exposed. He had got away with too much for too long.

Writing about him left a sour taste in Gisella's mouth and she pulled on a jacket. A walk would clear her head.

She had lost track of time while she was writing but, as she walked up the narrow country lane, she thought it must be late. A drizzle was falling but, wrapped up in her thoughts, she hardly noticed. The air smelt clean and the dampness settled on her cheeks like a mist. She wanted to walk on and on in the darkness without waking up to another day of knowing that Strachan could never love her.

She was halfway up the castle avenue before she realised where she was heading. For a moment she faltered, but something drove her on. Strachan was away; he would never know. What harm could it do? She would only look.

The drizzle had turned to rain, and she was sodden by the time the massive bulk of the castle rose out of the darkness before her. It looked curiously empty—or was that just because she knew Strachan wasn't there? Gisella forced herself not to wonder where he and Elspeth were or what they were doing together. To distract herself, she walked round to look up at the Candle Tower, and caught her breath.

A candle was burning in the window.

Rubbing her eyes, she looked again, certain that she must have imagined it, but it was still there, a single flame flickering high up in the dark tower.

Gisella stared at it in disbelief. She was a confirmed sceptic who had found a rational explanation for every one of the stories she had researched so far. If anything, she had thought that the story of the candle burning must have originated from a reflection, some trick of the light, but there it was, unmistakably a candle.

The flame guttered as if at a gust, and then recovered to burn even higher. Gisella watched it in fascination. It beckoned invitingly through the darkness and the rain and, without knowing quite why she did so, she began to walk towards it. She was at a side-door before she stopped. What on earth was she doing? She couldn't break into the castle like this! She couldn't see the flame from here and, losing her nerve, she stepped back until she could see it again.

It seemed to mock her for her cowardice. She had claimed that she wanted to see the tower, and now invitation beckoned irresistibly.

'If the door's open, I'll go in,' she decided, and found herself hoping that it would be locked as she reached out for the handle. But Strachan appeared to think that there was nothing worth stealing in the castle, for the door opened noiselessly and she stepped inside.

Telling herself that she would leave, Gisella none the less found herself in the great hall where the suits of armour loomed in the darkness and the grand staircase swept up to the shadowed gallery. A strange compulsion had taken hold of her, and she headed for the stairs as if in a dream. Her heart was beating faster, but she wasn't afraid.

Even so, she nearly screamed when a large shadow launched itself at her, and it was only when a wiry head thrust itself beneath her hand that she collapsed with relief.

'Bran!' Sinking down on to the stairs, she let him lick her while she steadied her nerves. 'A fine watch-dog you are!' she accused him. 'You're supposed to bark at intruders, not welcome them!' She ran her hand over him affectionately. She might not have been afraid, but it was strangely comforting to have him for company.

'Poor old thing,' she said sympathetically. 'Didn't Elspeth want you along for the weekend?' He was a little large to take around with you as a guest, she had to admit. Presumably Strachan had arranged for someone to feed and exercise him, and in the meantime he had been left to do a pretty poor job of guarding the castle!

Pushing Bran aside at last, she let him accompany her up the stairs and along the gallery, but he stopped at the oak door. He wagged his tail, but made it very obvious that he wasn't going any further.

'Coward!' Gisella whispered, even though she was tempted to stay with him.

But the memory of the burning candle lured her on and, pushing the door open resolutely, she began to climb the spiral staircase. The steps were very worn and she wondered how many people had trudged up as she was doing.

She was panting by the time she reached the top and she stood for a moment, trying to catch her breath. It was dark up here, but her eyes were well adjusted by now, and she could see that a screen had been placed at the entrance to the room, presumably to cut out the draughts.

Chewing her lip, she eyed the screen a little apprehensively, wondering what she was going to find on the other side. Of course, she didn't believe in ghosts, she reminded herself. It would just be an empty room with a candle burning in the window, and probably a twentieth-century room at that. Still she hesitated. She couldn't help thinking about all the films she had seen, when she had watched the heroine walk into danger all alone and had wanted to scream at her not to be so stupid, nobody in their right mind would do that.

And now here she was, proposing to do exactly the same thing!

She couldn't go back now. Taking a deep breath, Gisella walked round the screen. She found herself in a large room with three narrow windows spaced unevenly on the rounded outside wall. Their shutters closed out the night, but she could hear the moan of the wind as the rain threw itself at the glass panes. Above her, she could just make out a vaulted ceiling, and as her gaze travelled down she saw that the room was dominated by a heavy four-poster bed. It must have been built in here, she thought. It couldn't possibly have been carried up those stairs. Gaining confidence, Gisella moved forward, only to catch her jacket on the screen, which rocked and creaked alarmingly before settling back into place.

At that moment, there was a sleepy grunt from the bed and a bedside lamp clicked on, throwing a circle of warm light over the pillows.

Strachan McLeod had rolled on to his side. One hand was outstretched to the light, and the other was rubbing sleep from his eyes. It stopped abruptly as he took in the sight of Gisella, who was standing bedraggled by the screen, her grey eyes wide with shock, and the normally sleek hair hanging in limp rats' tails around her face.

For a moment there was utter silence as they stared at each other.

It was Gisella who found her voice first. 'I saw the candle,' she explained, too stunned by his sudden appearance to think clearly.

'The candle?' Strachan sounded understandably bemused.

'There was a candle burning in the window.'

Strachan looked at her as if she had gone mad. He probably thought she had. 'No, there wasn't.'

'But there was!' Gisella protested. 'I saw it!' She went over to the window and pulled back the shutters, but there was nothing there. No candle, no smell of melted wax, nothing.

She turned slowly back to face Strachan. 'I saw it,' she said again. She didn't seem to be able to say anything else.

He had pulled himself upright to watch her. His chest was bare and there was a curious expression on his face, but he said nothing.

Gisella swallowed. The candle had driven all other considerations from her mind, but now she realised what she had done. She had broken into his home and invaded his bedroom and disturbed his sleep.

'I thought you were away,' she explained in a small voice.

'I decided not to go,' he said.

'Oh.'

'I didn't want to spend the weekend with Elspeth and her friends.' Instead of being angry, he sounded as if he was excusing himself.

'Oh,' she said again.

Gisella was very conscious of the absurdity of the situation. There they were, making polite conversation, while he lay naked in his bed and she dripped on to the bare wooden floor, but everything seemed so unreal that she just stood and stared at him.

'You're wet,' he said at last.

She touched her hair as if noticing it for the first time. 'It's raining,' she explained a little unnecessarily as a fresh gust of wind rattled the panes and splattered rain against the glass.

'Take off your jacket,' he said, and nodded at a chair. 'There's a towel over there. Bring it here.' Moving over slightly, he patted the edge of the bed.

'But——'

'Don't argue, Gisella.' Strachan seemed to have adapted to the bizarre situation with ease and sounded almost normal. 'You're here, and now that you've gone to so much trouble you might as well stay. I certainly don't intend to get out of bed to take you home through the rain!'

'I can't stay,' she whispered.

'What?' he said, pretending to sound astonished. 'I thought that's what you'd been pestering me to allow you to do! Don't tell me that now you've finally got your own way, you're going to turn down the opportunity?'

'I shouldn't be here at all,' she muttered. 'You told me you didn't want me here.'

'I told you a lot of things I didn't really mean,' he said quietly. 'Now, come over here.'

Moving very slowly, as if in a dream, Gisella went and sat next to Strachan on the bed. He held out his hand for the towel and she gave it to him obediently. He dried her face as if she were a little girl and then rubbed her hair vigorously until she protested.

'What were you doing out in the rain?' he demanded with a touch of the old exasperation. 'You're soaked.'

'I was thinking.'

'What about?' He felt her hair to see if it were dry.

'About what a nuisance I'd been to you.' Gisella looked down at her hands, her eyelashes still spiky from the rain. 'I found out why you hate journalists so much. I didn't know before. I'm sorry. I thought you were just being bloody-minded. If I'd known I would never have hassled you the way I did.'

'And I would never have discovered that it's not possible to dislike every single journalist you come across, particularly when they've got eyes like woodsmoke on a summer evening and a smile that lights up the room . . .'

He made no move to touch her, but she knew that his eyes were on her downcast profile, and slowly she lifted her head to look at him. The expression in his eyes set her heart thudding with deep, almost painful strokes.

'I've been trying to convince myself since Wednesday that it *was* possible,' he went on reflectively. 'I told myself that you were only interested in your story, that you were too sophisticated and exasperating for me ever to like you, but it wasn't any good.' He paused and gave a wry smile, and then his voice deepened. 'I knew that if I ever touched you I'd be lost. I tried so hard not to lay myself open to temptation, but somehow you were always there with that defiant look in your eyes, being prickly and exasperating and utterly irresistible!'

A slow, incredulous smile had started in Gisella's eyes and trembled on the curve of her lips. 'I thought you despised me,' she said.

'I thought *you* despised *me*,' Strachan corrected her, and then he reached out and took her hand. 'Until I kissed you on Wednesday, and I thought you couldn't hate me that much, after all.'

Gisella's fingers curled around his. 'I didn't hate you at all. I don't think I ever did, but I did try, just like you!'

'We don't seem to have made a very good job of disliking each other, do we?'

'No.' A tingling glow of exquisite relief spread through her as she laughed with him, a soft, shared, secret laugh that crumbled the last of the barriers between them.

Strachan leant forward and took her face between his hands. 'You're very beautiful, Gisella. Ever since I kissed you, I've wanted to kiss you again, and now I'm going to. You don't mind, do you?'

'No,' said Gisella simply, knowing that there was nothing else she needed to say. Closing her eyes as his mouth found hers, she succumbed to a dizzying rush of happiness. It coursed through her veins as she opened her lips to his, tasting the sweetness and promise of his kiss.

'You are going to stay now, aren't you?' Strachan murmured against her throat, and she nodded, too full of emotion to speak.

Instead she slid from his grasp and stood up. He watched her in silence as she peeled off her clothes, but the look in his eyes when she stood naked before him made her blood sing in anticipation.

He lifted the sheet in mute invitation, and she slipped in beside him. The night was full of magic and it seemed quite natural to be lying here with him, as if the candle had beckoned her here on purpose. For a long moment they lay without even touching, just looking into each other's eyes, and then Strachan laid his hand against her cheek as if in wonderment.

Leaning over her, he kissed her mouth again, long, deep kisses, while Gisella tightened her arms around his neck and arched her body to the increasing demand of his hands. Her skin shuddered in exquisite torment at the touch of his hard male body, and when his lips left hers to begin a slow descent down her throat she gasped with pleasure.

He picked up her hand and buried a kiss in her palm before his mouth began a devastating exploration of her fragrant warmth, burning a trail up her arm, over the curve of her shoulder and along the seductive line of the clavicle. Gisella felt as if she was dissolving in a tide of sensation that rolled over her in wave upon wave of delight.

Abandoning herself utterly to his mouth and his hands and the tantalising feel of his skin, she wrapped herself around him and rained kisses where she could while she ran her hands over his taut body in breathless rapture.

'Gisella!' he mumbled against her breast. 'I've been thinking about this for weeks. I can't believe you're really here in my arms! It's like a dream, waking up and seeing you standing there, being able to hold you and touch you and feel you . . .' His lips and hands traced tantalising patterns on her tender warmth, circling her breasts in an ever decreasing spiral of desire until he found the taut peaks and teased them, nibbling and sucking until the strands at her core twisted in painful need.

Gisella's fingers dug into his shoulders as his kisses seared slowly, slowly, slowly downwards, and she whimpered his name, beyond coherent thought. Her body throbbed with need.

'Not yet.'

He continued his leisurely exploration, determined to touch and taste every inch of her silken skin, to discover each secret dip and curve and set every nerve tingling with desire. Only when his own need could no longer be denied did he retrace his way with increasing urgency, plundering her last reserves of control as he kissed her lips once more and possessed her with knowing hands that made Gisella sob in a frenzy of arousal.

'Please, Strachan!'

At last he relented, and as one they moved effortlessly together, but the urgency didn't disappear. Instead it grew and grew, gathering speed and height in a spiral of feeling so intense that it was almost painful. Locked together in passion, they urged each upwards until they could go no further and cried out in what sounded almost like despair.

For an eternal moment, they teetered on the edge of fulfilment, and then everything exploded in ecstasy and they were falling, tumbling down from the mind-stopping heights of rapture. They clung to each other through the first dizzying rush, but gradually the breathless fall slowed and they floated back to reality, their eyes dark and wide with wonder.

CHAPTER NINE

GISELLA nearly forgot to breathe. At the last moment she gave a deep, ragged sigh of utter bliss and opened her eyes.

Strachan lay on top of her, his face buried in her neck, and she wrapped her arms languorously about him and kissed his ear, which was the nearest bit of him she could find.

She felt him smile as he rolled over, taking her with him. Still entwined, still smiling, they lay and looked deeply into each other's eyes while their pulses steadied and their breathing returned to normal.

'I've changed my mind about the Lady Isobel,' Strachan said softly when he could speak. 'Perhaps she wasn't so bad, after all. If it hadn't been for her, you wouldn't be lying here now.'

'No.' Entangled in his arms, feeling him breathing against her, Gisella wondered if she had ever been happier. 'I really did see that candle, Strachan. It was almost as if it was beckoning me in.'

'Something must have known that I was lying here dreaming about you.' His lips found hers once more, but now the urgency had gone and their kisses were soft and warm. 'I've never believed all the stories about the castle being haunted before. It's strange that you should be the one to see the candle.

I thought you were coming here to debunk the story.'

'I was.' Gisella snuggled closer and he shifted slightly so she could rest her head in the hollow of his shoulder while he stroked her arm tenderly. 'It's ruined my article!' She felt him shake with silent laughter and she told him how Yvonne had been hassling her. 'That's why I was being so pushy,' she explained. 'I tried telling her how difficult you were, but she carried on as if the whole magazine would go under if I didn't get in here.'

'Well, here you are. She won't be able to complain that you haven't slept in the Candle Room when she gets your rewrite.' Strachan grinned at her expression as she pulled away to look at him.

'But... Won't you mind if I do the article?'

He shook his head. 'Not now. Not after tonight.' He stroked her hair as it gleamed in the lamplight. 'I've been bitter about journalists for long enough. Why shouldn't you write your story? It won't do anyone any harm.'

'Anyone would be bitter,' Gisella said softly. 'You must have felt so alone.'

'Yes, that's just what I did feel.' Strachan's arms tightened around her as he remembered. 'I suppose I felt my father had abandoned me along with everyone else. I was engaged to be married when it happened. Did you know that?'

Gisella nodded, but said nothing.

'Fay, her name was. She was beautiful. I can remember that without being able to tell you the colour of her eyes. She wanted to marry the heir to Kilnacroish, but a penniless laird from a disgraced family was a different matter.' He smiled, but without much humour. 'I wasn't very keen on women for a long time after that—until you came along, Gisella. There you were, everything I was determined not to fall for again, but I didn't stand a chance!'

Gisella smiled contentedly and kissed his neck. 'What about Elspeth?' she couldn't resist asking. 'You didn't seem to mind her!'

'Elspeth?' He shrugged a little uncomfortably. 'As far as I'm concerned, she's just a neighbour, but she has taken to dropping in rather a lot recently. I've tried to discourage her, but I can hardly stop her bumping into me on market day, or turning up at the same parties, can I?'

Gisella thought that she could think of a few ways, but she kept them to herself. 'It's hardly discouraging her to agree to go away with her for the weekend,' she pointed out. 'Mrs Robertson told me you'd gone off together.'

'Mrs Robertson is a terrible gossip,' Strachan said severely. 'Elspeth kept inviting me to join their shooting parties—hardly a weekend for two! I'd put it off as long as I could, but in the end I simply ran out of excuses. She asked me months ago when I could make it, so I had to give in and suggest this weekend. Last week, I even thought I would go in the hope that it would distract me from thinking about you, but I rang her up at the last minute and told her I wouldn't be able to make it after all. I didn't want to spend a whole weekend with the Drummonds and their friends where there was no chance of seeing you.'

'I thought you were in love with her,' Gisella confessed. 'She always behaves as if she's about to become the lady of the castle. Look at the way she followed you into the gallery the other night.'

'I was furious with her for interrupting,' said Strachan. 'Nearly as furious as I was with myself for kissing you! I was lost by then, and I knew it.'

'Is that why you told her that kissing me was nothing important?'

'I just wanted to get her out of the gallery. It wouldn't have taken her long to see what we'd been doing, and I knew that if I stayed anywhere near you I'd end up kissing you again, no matter who saw us.'

Gisella pulled herself up so that she could lean over him, the golden hair falling softly forward to sweep against his cheeks. 'Like this?' she asked, and brushed her mouth tantalisingly over his lips.

'Like *this*,' he corrected and pulled her down for a long, deep kiss.

Gisella sighed happily as she emerged breathless at last. 'I didn't think I stood a chance against Elspeth,' she said. 'She's so suitable for you.'

'Bran doesn't think so,' Strachan said, running his hand over the enticing curve of her hip in warm possession. 'He never liked Elspeth. In fact, he's never liked women much at all. That's why I was so surprised when he took to you. He knew before I did that you were the right girl for me, in spite of everything.'

'I wasn't always,' she admitted. 'I was an investigative reporter, and a good one. I wrote about stories I thought needed to be told, but a few months ago I found I'd had enough of writing about so much corruption and incompetence. I won't do any more investigative work now.'

Strachan brought her close to him once more. 'Someone has to do it, you're right. I resented the way my father's affairs were reported, but the fact was that he was in the wrong. He ruined himself, and he ruined Kilnacroish.'

'Has it been a terrible struggle?'

'It's been hard work,' he said, and the simple words told Gisella as much as she needed to know about the years he had battled alone to keep the estate going. 'I learnt who my real friends were, and I've survived. I hate seeing the castle falling into disrepair, but I won't sell it. This is my home.'

'Will you ever be able to repair it?' she asked.

'I hope so. Now that the estate is back on its feet, I'm trying to think of ways to bring in some extra money. I want to set up an outdoor activities centre so that other people can enjoy the land as well, but I'm still waiting for planning permission.' He sighed. 'If they refuse permission, I'll be back at square one.'

'Why should they?' asked Gisella. 'It sounds a good idea to me.'

'This is all conservation land round here. They're not keen on letting people build on it.' Strachan frowned, and then shrugged off his worries. Tangling his fingers in her hair, he smiled down at her. 'Funnily enough, it doesn't seem such a big problem right at this moment! The castle could collapse about my ears and it wouldn't matter if you were with me.' His face changed and became suddenly serious. 'Nothing would matter if you were with me, Gisella. Will you stay?'

'As long as you want me,' she promised quietly, and he gathered her to him, the dawning smile of relief in his eyes making her heart contract with love.

'Forever? Will you stay forever?'

'Yes.'

'You mean you'll marry me? You're prepared to live in a crumbling castle with no heating and rain dripping through the roof?'

'Yes.' She laughed at him, alight with joy. 'As long as you promise to keep me warm.'

He pulled her tight against him. 'It'll be a pleasure!' he whispered, just before their lips met in a kiss that pledged a lifetime of love. It began in tenderness and when it changed neither of them could tell, but imperceptibly the glow between them flickered into flames once more and, as it burnt higher, they succumbed to its insistence and let their bodies move in timeless delight until together they rediscovered the soaring heights of passion.

The next morning, Strachan made her toast and coffee for breakfast in the vast, echoing kitchen. Gisella sat at the scrubbed pine table and watched him with shining eyes. A night of love and little sleep had left her in a state of euphoria and, after the enchanted, dream-like quality of the night, the morning was bright and clear. Even the sun was shining.

She looked around her with new eyes, as if the world had taken on a new definition overnight, leaving everything somehow more solid and distinct. Two blackened ranges stretched along one wall of the kitchen and the biggest dresser she had ever seen along another. An old-fashioned fridge rattled in the corner, and the flagstones underfoot were worn and hollowed with age.

'It's not exactly streamlined, is it?' Strachan said, setting the coffee down in front of her.

Gisella grinned. 'Not exactly!'

'In fact, it's not much of a home to offer you.' Strachan looked about him with a grimace as he sat down opposite her. 'Damp, rotting, cold...sure you don't want to change your mind?'

'No.' She shook her head, and then glanced down at Bran, who had greeted them both ecstatically at the foot of the staircase that morning and was sitting at her feet. 'Besides, I've promised Bran that I'll stay.'

'So you'll marry me and come and live in all this?'

She reached across the table and laid her hand against his cheek with a smile. 'Yes,' she said. 'I'll live anywhere with you.'

Strachan captured her hand and looked across at her, with such warmth in his eyes that her heart almost failed her. 'Did I tell you how much I love you, Gisella?'

'Do you know, I don't think you did!'

'Well, I do.' He leant over and kissed her. 'Do you love me?'

'You know I do.'

They sat over their breakfast, until Strachan reluctantly decided that he would have to go out and check on his stock. 'Those stalking cattle that so alarmed you!' he explained, and Gisella laughed. Only yesterday she had thought she would never laugh again.

'They don't need any looking after...they can look after themselves!'

She had planned to take her story on William Ross into Crieston to show Iain Douglas, but when Strachan offered to drive her back to the cottage to fetch her car she shook her head.

'I'd like to walk. It's such a lovely morning.'

Outside, the ground was covered in a glittering layer of frost. The sky was a duck-egg blue and the air was exhilaratingly crisp and cold. Across the river, the hills seemed very close, and stood out in almost unnatural clarity in shades of gold and brown. Bran snuffled joyously across the frosty lawn in search of rabbits.

Strachan took Gisella's face between his hands. 'Will you come back later?'

'I'll come and cook you supper,' she promised with a smile.

He pulled her close for a goodbye kiss that lingered on and on, both of them reluctant to be the first to break away. 'I must go,' Gisella mumbled, but made no protest when Strachan kissed her again.

Absorbed in each other, they didn't notice the car drive up until it tooted its horn, and they jumped apart in surprise.

Mrs McInnes leant out of the driver's window, her bright eyes speculative. 'I just thought I'd come and let you know how much money we made last Wednesday, Strachan, but I can see that I'm interrupting…' She smiled archly at Gisella who found, much to her chagrin, that she was blushing.

'I'm just going,' she said quickly. 'I'll see you later, Strachan.' It *would* be Mrs McInnes, she thought as she hurried down the avenue. By lunchtime, everyone would know that she had spent the night with him!

But what did it matter? On this beautiful morning, with her body still glowing from a night of love, Gisella was gloriously happy. The parting look Strachan had given her sent her blood singing through her veins. She was walking on air. She wanted to burst into song and swing around lampposts.

She floated into Crieston and scoured the shops for an intimate dinner for two. Then she composed her face into a suitably professional expression to hand in her story to Iain Douglas, but kept breaking into idiotic smiles as he read it.

'What's happened to you?' he asked in some amusement. 'You're lit up like a Christmas tree!'

'Just enjoying the beautiful weather,' Gisella assured him gaily. She and Strachan had agreed that they would keep their engagement to themselves for a while. When Iain showed his disbelief, she changed the subject quickly. 'What do you think of my piece?'

'Brilliant!' he congratulated her. 'You're a sharp writer, and you've certainly nailed Ross. There'll be uproar on Thursday when this is splashed all over the front page!' He contemplated the prospect with satisfaction. 'Everyone will want a copy of the *Echo*!'

'I hope it helps the Donalds, that's all.'

'It will,' Iain reassured her. 'There'll be such an outcry when people learn that he's trying to evict an old couple just so that he can build a luxurious health farm that no one around here will be able to afford to use, the planners won't dare give him permission to go ahead.'

He offered her a celebratory drink, but Gisella was eager to get back to Kilnacroish. Waving goodbye, she ran eagerly down the stairs and almost bumped into Alan Wates. She was about to apologise when she saw that Elspeth Drummond was with him.

'Hello,' she said with a smile. Now that she knew she didn't have to be jealous of Elspeth, it was easy to be nice. She could even feel sorry for her.

Elspeth muttered a greeting in reply, eyeing Gisella's radiant face with sullen dislike, and Alan looked equally displeased to see her.

They were well suited, Gisella thought as she walked back to the car, but their hostility meant nothing to her today. Strachan loved her, that was all that mattered.

The days that followed were halcyon ones for Gisella. She rewrote the article for Yvonne, sitting in the Candle Tower itself, hunched over the typewriter with three jumpers on and a scarf wrapped round her neck. She had to keep stopping to blow on her numb fingers but, when she had finished, she knew that it was one of the best articles she had ever written.

Yvonne was jubilant. 'I knew you could do it, Gisella! Even the editor commented on how good your piece was! Tremendous atmosphere, too. That castle sounds like quite a place. No wonder your grumpy old laird doesn't want to share it—it must be nice to have a place like that to yourself.'

Gisella glanced affectionately around the shabby library. 'It is,' she said.

Once she had sent the finished article off to Yvonne, she was free to explore the castle. She had felt drawn to it the first time she had seen it, and the feeling grew as she wandered from room to room, up and down the stone stairways and along the contorted corridors. It was a desperately inconvenient and uncomfortable place to live, but Gisella was enchanted and her fingers itched to bring the neglected rooms back to life.

Strachan took her round the estate, and she even learnt to tramp fearlessly through fields of bullocks, with the man and the dog as protection on either side. 'We'll make a farmer's wife of you yet,' Strachan grinned as he helped her over a dike.

Her senses still thrilled at the merest touch, and he always knew. He would catch her eye, and his hold would tighten, and she would tense with anticipation. It didn't matter where they were. In the car, in the woods, in the steadings, their eyes would meet in secret knowledge and reality would fade into breathless excitement. Bran frequently got bored at these unscheduled stops, and had to bark to break them apart, laughing and careless of what anyone else might think.

'I never get any work done when you're around,' Strachan told her with mock severity. 'You're much too distracting. Bran thinks you should stay at home!'

In the evenings, they would build up the fire in the library, and plan a golden future together, Strachan sitting in his chair and Gisella on the floor, leaning against his knees. He was confident that the outdoor centre would be a success, if he could only get planning permission, and when Gisella saw the plans he had drawn up she began to share his excitement.

The future was absorbing, but it was easy to be diverted by the present when they were alone with the firelight and each other. Gisella would look up from the papers and see Strachan watching her with a smile in his eyes. No words were needed as she slid on to his lap and gave herself up to the exquisite delight of his kisses, and by unspoken agreement they would cross the hall and climb the stone stairs to the Candle Tower.

If the days were full of joy, the nights were enchanted. They loved each other with a passion that left Gisella awed and amazed, sometimes shaken, at the new realms of feeling they discovered together.

By the time Friday came, she had almost forgotten about her front page story. Strachan had to go into Crieston, but Gisella stayed to help Mrs Robertson get ready for the ball that night.

'I'd forgotten all about it,' Strachan confessed when Mrs Robertson reminded him.

'Aye, well, you've other things on your mind,' she said indulgently. She was cock-a-hoop to find Gisella installed where she had dreaded seeing

Elspeth, and kept dropping broad hints about wedding bells.

Together Gisella and Mrs Robertson prepared a mountain of food to lay on great trestle-tables, and enjoyed a cosy gossip. Mrs Robertson had come in just after Strachan had left, waving her copy of the *Echo*. 'What a story!' she chortled. 'That man Ross will never dare show his face around here again! You've saved the Donalds for sure!'

Gisella scanned the front page. The story was splashed just as Iain had promised, and she had been given a prominent byline. Pleased, she laid the paper aside without glancing any further. They still had a lot to do before everyone arrived that evening. She was not allowed to forget it, though. Everyone, it seemed, wanted to ring her up and congratulate her on the story. Many of them had their own grievances against Ross which they had never dared air before, and they thanked her effusively for bringing it all out into the open.

'You're a heroine!' Mrs Robertson said proudly as she buttered the bridge rolls.

Gisella just laughed. She was delighted with the reaction, but her mind was more occupied with memories of the previous night and eager anticipation of the night to come. Everyone seemed determined to come and enjoy the ball, so she would too, but she knew it would seem a long, long evening until she and Strachan were left alone again.

She had just taken the last of the quiches out of the oven when she heard Strachan's Land Rover crunching over the gravel outside. Her hands still encased in oven mitts, she went along to the hall to greet him away from Mrs Robertson's intensely interested gaze.

'Hello!' she said, going towards him with a smile. She waved a mitt at the trestle-tables, which were already groaning with food. They had polished up the armour and decorated the hall as best they could, so that it had a festive air. 'What do you think? It looks good, doesn't it?' She stopped, aware suddenly that Strachan's face was grim and shuttered, and a cold finger of fear touched her heart. 'What's the matter?'

'I bought the *Echo* in town,' he said in a voice so bitter that she hardly recognised it. He shook the paper at her. 'I suppose you're feeling pretty pleased with yourself?'

Gisella could see the headline: 'Local Couple Evicted For Ross Health Farm.' 'Well, yes, I am,' she admitted, seeing no reason to be ashamed of helping the Donalds. She couldn't imagine why Strachan was so angry about it.

'And you had the gall to tell me you were tired of investigative work! Was that the only lie you told me, or has it all been lies?'

Gisella stared at him in shock. 'I haven't lied to you! I *am* tired of writing those kind of pieces, but if you've read it you'll know why I couldn't pass the story up.'

'No, you can never pass up a good story, can you, Gisella?' Strachan said savagely. 'It doesn't matter what you have to do to get it! Not that you had to do very much to get *this* story, did you?'

'It wasn't that difficult to find out the information,' Gisella said, still baffled.

'I'll bet! Seducing some poor, besotted fool is all in a day's work for you!'

'Seducing...?' Gisella was beginning to get angry herself. 'I've only ever spoken to William Ross on the phone to get his comments, and he was far from being seduced, I can tell you.'

'I'm not talking about William Ross, and you know it!'

'Well, what *are* you talking about?'

'This.' Strachan unfolded the paper and shoved page two under her nose. 'Storm Brewing Over Laird's Plans For Beauty Spot,' ran the headline, above a photograph of the castle and a detailed description of his plans. People were up in arms, claimed the article, at the prospect of such a valuable ecological site being used for such a scheme.

Gisella's grey eyes widened in shock. 'But how did they find out about it?'

'How indeed!' Strachan said bitterly, jabbing his finger at the byline.

She had been so busy reading the article that she hadn't noticed it before, but now her jaw dropped as she stared, appalled, at the name that danced before her eyes. 'By Gisella Pryde and Alan Wates.'

'But I didn't write this!'

'Don't try and act the innocent!' said Strachan, savagely. 'All those evenings talking about the centre, studying the plans...you were thinking about this story all along, weren't you?'

Gisella felt as if she were living in a nightmare. 'Of course I wasn't! I told you, there's been some mistake. The article's nothing to do with me,' she cried in desperation. 'I didn't even know about the centre until you told me.'

'Don't lie, Gisella. You've been spending a lot of time in the planning office lately, I've been told. Where better to find out whose plans you can ruin by spilling the story too early?'

Her hands were shaking, and she realised that she was still wearing the oven mitts. Tugging them off, she clenched her fingers around them in an effort to keep control.

'Yes, I've been in the planning office. There's no secret about it. I was trying to find out about William Ross's plans for the Donalds' cottage—I told you about that!'

'And was William Ross the reason you were so keen to get into the castle? You've had plenty of opportunity to go through my papers over the last few days.' He threw the paper against the wall and it fell on to the floor, scattering pages. 'What a fool I've been! If anyone should have known never to trust a journalist, it should have been me, but no! A warm body, a pair of grey eyes, and I was hooked as surely as anyone else. I believed every word you said!' He grabbed Gisella by the shoulders and shook her in his fury, so that the golden hair tumbled about her face. 'All this time I've trusted you, and you've been laughing at me, haven't you? *Haven't you*?'

Incandescent with rage, Gisella pulled herself from his grasp. 'How dare you even *think* that of me? Do you really think I'd go to all the trouble of seducing you just for one crummy story about a perfectly inoffensive outdoor centre? It's not even a good story!' Bran whined in distress at the raised, angry voices, but they both ignored him.

'It doesn't matter whether it's good enough. It'll still torpedo the whole plan. As soon as the planners clap eyes on the story, they'll refuse permission out of hand for the centre.'

'Rubbish! If it were that big a story, they'd have put it on the front page. As it's on page two, it's just filling space!' Gisella retrieved the page from the floor and scanned the article scornfully. 'Why on earth should I bother to write a story like this? I wouldn't demean myself! It's badly written and inaccurate and, if you'd bothered to compare the two stories, you'd have known that I couldn't possibly have written it!'

'Perhaps Alan Wates wrote it, with in-depth research from the famous Miss Pryde,' Strachan suggested angrily.

Gisella's eyes were dark with fury. 'You're determined not to believe me, aren't you? After all we've meant to each other over the past few days, you can really believe this of me! How could you?' She was too angry to cry. 'If you really loved me, you would have known immediately that I couldn't possibly have written this, but you weren't going to give up on all your old prejudices that easily, were you? It's much easier to believe that I'm a wicked journalist—worse, a wicked woman journalist—than to trust me! Well, if that's the way you want it, that's fine, but don't expect me to hang around and wait for you to discover how wrong you are! I'm leaving right now!'

CHAPTER TEN

THROWING the oven mitts at him in furious despair, Gisella turned towards the door, determined to walk out there and then, but Strachan's arm shot out and caught her in an iron grip.

'Oh, no, you don't! I'm not being publicly jilted by another fiancée!'

'Nobody knows that we're engaged . . . that we *were* engaged,' she corrected herself coldly.

'That's what you think! Between them, Mrs Robertson and Mrs McInnes seemed to have informed the whole district about us. Three people even congratulated me to my face in town today, and the others contented themselves with nudges and winks. They're all coming here tonight expecting to see you here as my fiancée, and that's what they *will* see.'

'Why can't you tell them we've had an argument?' she demanded, incensed. 'It's the truth, after all!'

Strachan shook his head. 'No. Everyone round here looks forward to the ball, and if they think we've had a row they'll feel embarrassed and won't enjoy themselves. I've had a lot of sympathy over the years for the way Fay treated me, and I won't spoil their evening tonight.'

'I'm glad you've got so much consideration for their feelings!' Gisella snapped. 'What about mine?'

'What feelings?' he retorted bitterly. 'Anyone who can use a man the way you used me doesn't have any feelings.'

'You certainly haven't got any! You've just got prejudices!' Gisella managed to wrench her arm free at last. 'Can you give me one reason why I should stay and save face for you after the things you've said to me?'

'You owe me,' he said flatly. 'You've got what you wanted, now you can pay for it. It's not as if you hadn't had any practice at pretence! We'll tell people that we're not engaged, of course, but they won't believe us. One evening, that's all I ask, and then I'll be glad to see you go.'

Before Gisella could reply, a vehicle came crunching to a halt on to the forecourt outside. Doors banged and voices shouted to each other in cheerful contrast to the tension inside the hall.

'This is the band,' Strachan said, glancing out of the narrow window. 'They've come early to set up a platform.' He looked back at Gisella, who was standing rigid with anger, her grey eyes blazing defiance. 'I trust you'll have the common decency to behave as if nothing had happened in front of other people?'

Gisella clenched her fists. 'Don't worry, even journalists know how to behave sometimes!' She tore off her apron and dropped it on the floor at his feet before swinging round and stalking towards the staircase. 'You can finish the cooking yourself.'

'Where are you going?' he demanded sharply.

'You want me to look like a fiancée, don't you?' She stopped at the top of the first flight of stairs where they turned up to the gallery, her hand on the ornately carved banister. 'I'm going upstairs to change.'

She ran along the gallery and up the stone steps to the tower, slamming the great oak door behind her. The Candle Tower looked just the same, as she stood panting at the top of the steps. There was the bed where they had spent so many sweet hours. Only this morning, Strachan had wakened her with kisses and lazily drifting hands. How could things have gone wrong so quickly?

Gisella was seized by an icy anger that gripped her heart and froze the tears in her eyes. She ran herself a bath, deliberately using all the hot water so that Strachan would have to wash in cold. It served him right for being so pig-headed and suspicious! How *could* he have thought she would do anything like that? she raged inwardly. Hadn't he learnt anything about her these last few days? He was lucky she hadn't walked out on him there and then!

She would help him save face this evening, but tomorrow she was definitely leaving! She must have been mad to fall in love with a man so obstinately biased and embittered! Remembering the things he had said to her, Gisella made herself up in a fury. If Strachan determined that she was wicked and deceitful, that was how she would look!

Dimly, she recognised that her anger was her only defence against the tide of misery that threatened to overwhelm her, and she kept it kindled by reminding herself how unfair and distrustful Strachan had been.

By the time she got back to the Candle Tower, he had clearly been and gone, for his clothes had been tossed on to the bed as if he had changed in a fury as great as her own. The sight of the crumpled shirt and trousers reminded Gisella of the times he had pulled off his clothes with a grin before climbing into bed beside her, and her heart twisted painfully at the memory.

She turned away, folding her lips firmly together to stop their trembling. If he was capable of pretending that nothing had happened to a roomful of people, so was she!

Dressing quickly, Gisella studied her reflection in the long cheval-glass. In the dim light, her face had a wild, witchy look and her eyes gleamed with suppressed emotion. Her shoulders were bare and cold above the strapless dress. She shivered, but had no intention of changing out of such an eye-catching outfit. The vivid sea-green colour and full, swinging skirt flattered her figure, and if she looked unsuitably dramatic for a local ball, so much the better! Even if she wasn't staying, she would make sure they all remembered her!

It sounded as if the party was well on its way by the time she made her way back down the stairs. She could hear the accordionist warming up, and a hubbub of chatter from the arriving guests. Peering out of an upstairs window, Gisella saw that the forecourt was full of cars. People were parking all the way down the avenue, and walking up the drive in laughing groups, their feet crunching on the frosty gravel, and their breath hanging in white clouds on the cold, clear air.

Beneath a starry winter sky, the frozen countryside lay stark and still. The only warmth came from the castle lights, which threw yellow rectangles of warmth across the forecourt. The front door was open, spilling out laughter and the gay sound of the fiddle into the night.

As she looked down on the happy scene, Gisella's heart felt like a stone. She had been happy too until a couple of hours ago. Now it was hard to remember that she had ever been anything but furiously, bitterly angry.

She paused at the top of the stairs. Below her, the great hall was full of people. At one end of the hall, the band had established themselves on a platform and were drinking beer while they tuned up, and the fire blazed at the other. It threw out such a heat that the semicircle round it stood well back, their faces bathed in the red glow of the flames.

Mrs Robertson had told her that the ball was a very informal affair, but many of the men were in kilts. Some wore them casually with just a shirt, others were more traditionally attired in waistcoats and short jackets, their buttons a-gleam. Next to them, the women seemed dull but, even so, the hall was a vivid kaleidoscope of colour: reds and greens and blues, interspersed with the stark elegance of black and white and the occasional flash of a gold button or a silver sash brooch.

Gisella's eyes searched the blur of faces until she found Strachan. In spite of her anger, her heart turned over at the sight of him. He was standing near the door, the dark, austere features lit by a smile as he greeted new arrivals. He didn't look as if his heart was breaking, Gisella thought, and her chin went up. Had he simply realised how unsuitable a wife she would be and used the article as an excuse to break everything off?

Strachan turned from the door to point someone towards the table of drinks and, as he did so, he looked up and saw her watching him. Those near him turned their heads to see what held his gaze so intently, and conversation trailed away into expectant silence across the hall as they all looked up at the vivid girl standing at the top of the stairs.

Gisella swallowed. Taking a deep breath, she began to walk very carefully down the stairs into the silence. There was a stir of interest as Strachan began to make his way through the crowd to meet her, but Mrs Donald got there first.

As Gisella reached the bottom, the old lady pushed forward and threw her arms around her. 'I can't thank you enough, Gisella,' she said, almost incoherent with gratitude. 'The agent rang us today and said that we'd be able to stay in the cottage after all, and such a nice man came from the council and said that now they'd read your story they'd make sure we were all right, no matter what happened.' She hugged Gisella again. 'It's all thanks to you. If you hadn't found out what Mr Ross was up to, I don't know what we'd have done.'

Gisella forced a smile and hugged Mrs Donald back. 'I'm so glad everything has worked out.'

'Archie wants to thank you, too,' Mrs Donald said, and beckoned to her husband.

He wheeled himself forward in his chair, a dour, taciturn-looking man who eyed Gisella apprais-ingly. He seemed to approve of what he saw, for he smiled suddenly and held out a gnarled hand. It was a surprisingly sweet smile, and stupidly Gisella felt tears sting her eyes as the cold hand of misery around her heart eased its grip slightly. On an impulse, she bent and kissed Archie Donald's leathery cheek.

There was an approving murmur near by and, as if at a signal, conversation broke out around the hall once more, and the fiddler resumed his tuning.

Gisella straightened to find Strachan watching her with a blaze of expression in his eyes, quickly shuttered. He hadn't forgiven her, she realised, and the misery tightened its fingers so that they dug into her heart once more.

'She's a fine lassie,' Archie said to Strachan, whose mouth twisted in a bitter smile.

'I know.'

'We're all very glad to hear the good news,' Mrs Donald added, beaming as she looked from Strachan to Gisella. Mrs Robertson had evidently been keeping her fully informed of the situation.

Strachan glanced at Gisella, who was standing rigidly beside him. 'We don't have any definite plans,' he said, but Mrs Donald was not to be discouraged.

'It's high time you did, then!' she scolded him. 'I might be a foolish old lady, but you only have to look at you to see that you're in love!'

As they made their way doggedly around the room, Gisella and Strachan had to listen to everyone saying much the same thing. Their denials of an engagement were met with knowing looks and conspiratorial winks, and they had to endure fulsome congratulations, Gisella for exposing William Ross's treatment of the Donalds, and Strachan for his plans for the outdoor centre.

'It's a marvellous idea,' they all told him. It was soon clear that most people had read the article uncritically, and were more taken with the idea of a facility that could be used by local people than worried by its ecological drawbacks. They were sure they could rely on their laird not to be putting up any eyesores. William Ross was notably absent, but there were plenty of other local councillors there, who clapped Strachan on the shoulder and told him they were glad that he had gone public with his plans. 'There's a lot of support locally,' they said. 'You don't need to worry about planning permission. We'll make sure it goes through all right.'

It was ironic that the story which had broken their happiness should ensure the success of the centre Strachan so badly needed, Gisella thought, and she wondered whether it would change his attitude. Somehow she doubted it. He still thought that she was capable of deceit and betrayal and, as long as he did, there was no future for them together.

Closing her heart once more, Gisella pinned a bright smile to her face, and let Strachan do the talking. They didn't look at each other and they didn't touch, but she was very conscious of him beside her. Surely the tension between them must make it obvious to everyone that they were far from being engaged?

Her jaw began to ache with the effort of smiling, and she was relieved when Meg pounced on her and drew her aside.

'What's all this I hear?' she demanded. 'People keep telling me that you and Strachan are engaged! You might have told me about it! I'm supposed to be your friend!'

'We're not engaged,' Gisella said wearily, as she had so many times already this evening.

'Everyone else seems to think you are!'

Gisella glanced over her shoulder. Strachan was listening courteously to an elderly lady but, as if aware of her gaze, he looked up and met her eyes through the crowd. Her heart jolted and she turned quickly back to Meg.

'We did think about it,' she admitted, 'but we've both realised that it would be a terrible mistake.'

The pain in Gisella's grey eyes shocked Meg out of her teasing mood. 'It's not a mistake to marry someone you love,' she said.

'It is when you don't trust them.' Gisella's voice was bitter.

Meg looked at her with concern. 'Why don't you trust Strachan? He's obviously madly in love with you.'

'Not any more, he isn't,' Gisella said. 'And he's the one who doesn't trust me!'

'That's right, I don't,' Strachan said coolly, appearing at her side. 'Have you been telling Meg how you took me for a ride?'

'No, but I was about to tell her how bigoted and unreasonable you are!' Gisella snapped, alarmed by the treacherous way her senses leapt at his presence, and determined not to show it.

'Better than being a pushy journalist!' he retorted.

They glared at each other, and Meg's worried look vanished as she saw how they were aware only of each other. 'Now, now, children,' she soothed. 'Play nicely!'

Strachan looked cross, as if Gisella had provoked him into revealing far more than he wanted. 'Excuse us, will you, Meg?' he said quickly, taking Gisella's wrist in a firm grip. 'Gisella and I need to start the reels.'

'What if I don't want to dance?' Gisella protested angrily.

'Everyone's expecting us to start the dancing together. Come along, and for God's sake look as if you're enjoying yourself!'

'I'm not enjoying myself,' she grumbled. 'And I can't possibly dance with you. I don't know the steps.'

'Just watch what everyone else does.' Strachan nodded at the band, who had been waiting for his signal, and the accordionist caught everyone's attention with a long chord quavering with anticipation. Obediently the crowd drifted towards the edges of the hall to clear a space in the middle for the dancing.

It seemed to Gisella that she and Strachan stood alone in the middle of the floor for an age, keeping a good distance between them and studiously ignoring each other, while the rest found partners and gradually formed up into a set. There was much laughter and good-natured jostling as the sets shuffled out to form two circles, but she felt isolated from it all.

Strachan was laughing at something the girl on his other side was saying; no one would guess that he was supposed to be dancing with *her*, Gisella thought crossly. She knew that she should talk to the man next to her, but she could only think about Strachan and the way his body was turned away from hers.

At last the band struck the long opening chord, and they all joined hands. Gisella took a deep breath as Strachan's strong fingers closed over hers, and tried to concentrate on the dance.

'Smile!' Strachan ordered her out of the side of his mouth as they circled round to the left, and then back to the right.

'I'm trying to watch what's going on,' she whispered back furiously. 'You're the one who wanted me to join in your rotten dance!'

All too soon it was her turn to dance in the middle of the circle while the others circled round her, all beaming approvingly except for Strachan. Fortunately, Gisella had a natural sense of rhythm, and it was easy enough to pick up the '*pas de bas*' step, but she got hopelessly confused when the circling stopped and she was expected to start turning the men as she had seen the others do.

'Concentrate, Gisella!' Strachan hissed, solving her problem by taking her hands and swinging her round him. 'Why haven't you been watching the other girls? They didn't stand around looking vacantly at their partners!'

Gisella flushed. 'That's probably because their partners weren't ignoring them!' she retorted, just before he dropped her hands and sent her hurtling over to the man on the opposite side of the circle.

'You're a fine one to talk about ignoring!' he muttered, when she had turned the other men and gratefully resumed her place in the circle. 'You're supposed to be happy, but you've hardly said a word to me.' He took her hand and they circled to the left once more with fixed smiles.

'I didn't know what your back would be interested in hearing!' Gisella snapped. 'Your front seemed to be engrossed in that rather pretty brunette on your other side!'

'I'm only being sociable,' he whispered back. 'I am the host, after all, and it would look extremely strange if I stood around sulking like you! You're not giving a very good impression of a girl who's just got engaged!'

'I wonder why that is?' she muttered sarcastically.

Gisella thought it would never end, but somehow they got through the reel—dancing when required, clapping when required, swinging when required—both wearing bright, brittle smiles.

She was panting with exertion by the time they had finished. Abandoning Strachan to the congratulations of yet another delighted couple, she fought her way through the crowd for some cool air. She had never thought she would feel hot in this hall!

'Gisella!' Iain Douglas waved a hand in front of her face to attract her attention. 'That was a great story you did for us! Everyone's talking about it and the *Echo*'s sold out! There's even going to be a special investigation into Ross as a result of your report.'

'Oh, good,' said Gisella listlessly.

'The story on page two had nearly as much interest,' Iain went on, not noticing her lack of enthusiasm. 'By the way, did you notice we put your byline on after all?'

'Someone did point it out to me,' she said with an edge to her voice. 'Why did you do it, Iain?'

'Well, Alan came to me and told me he wanted to do the story,' he confided. 'Frankly, I thought he'd had his nose put out of joint by your success, so I was really pleased when he told me that he'd decided to try and take advantage of your experience and work with you rather than against you. He said you'd given him lots of good advice and, although you'd told him not to give you any credit, he really felt you deserved a byline for all your help, so of course I was happy to oblige.'

Why had Alan lied? Gisella wasn't even sure she cared any more. She looked down at her hands and wondered what he would say if she told him what heartache Alan's lie had caused. But what good would it do? It wasn't Iain's fault that Strachan was so ready to think the worst of her.

Suddenly, she badly needed to be alone. Smiling mechanically, she slipped through the press of people to the door, which still stood open to let in some cool air. It was a relief to get outside and stop smiling. She leant against the cold stone and closed her eyes, letting the chill air calm the flush on her skin.

'You don't look very happy for a girl who's supposedly just got engaged.'

Gisella opened her eyes to see Elspeth Drummond regarding her with some satisfaction. She was wearing a white blouse with a frilly neck and a long tartan skirt that made Gisella's dress look garish and unsuitable.

'I knew it wouldn't last, of course,' Elspeth went on. 'Strachan might have fallen for you for a while, but you're the wrong kind of girl for him, and he knows it. His fiancée was a flashy English city girl, like you, and she wouldn't have belonged here any more than you do. He needs a country girl.'

'Like you, I suppose?'

Elspeth flushed. 'Yes, like me. We were almost engaged before you came along and spoilt everything.'

'I don't believe you,' Gisella said in a level voice. 'You might have wanted Strachan to be in love with you, but he wasn't. He fell in love with me instead.'

'He doesn't seem very in love with you now,' Elspeth tittered angrily. 'It was stupid of you to write that story about his outdoor centre, wasn't it? He wouldn't have liked you spilling his secrets to the papers.'

Gisella hugged her arms together against the cold. 'I didn't write the story. Somebody else gave Alan the details about the centre, and put my name on it.' She looked at Elspeth with dawning suspicion, remembering how she had seen her and Alan Wates going into the *Echo* office together. 'You wouldn't know who that someone would be, would you, Elspeth?'

'Me?' Elspeth looked wary. 'How should I know?'

'You know Alan Wates.'

'Strachan never told me about his plans for the centre, though,' Elspeth said triumphantly. 'Ask him if you don't believe me!'

'Rather strange that he never mentioned it to you when you were "almost engaged",' Gisella flashed back. 'Anyway, he wouldn't need to have told you. He told me himself that you were always dropping in, and the castle's never locked. You could easily have found his papers and seen what he was planning.'

'What if I did?' Elspeth demanded, suddenly shrill. 'Everything was perfect till you came along. Strachan was happy as he was. I saw him kiss you the other night, and I knew you'd trap him if you could. Old Mrs McInnes took great pleasure in telling me that you'd spent the night with him, so I rang Alan and told him I had a story for him as long as he said you had helped him. I knew Strachan hated reporters, and it wouldn't take much to persuade him that you'd given the story to the paper.' Elspeth gave a smug smile as she saw Gisella's expression. 'Alan wasn't too keen to give you any extra credit at first, but he was so desperate for a story to match yours that he gave in in the end. I told him what I knew about the centre, and he made up the rest,' she finished casually.

Gisella could hardly believe what she was hearing. 'Didn't it occur to you that you were jeopardising all Strachan's plans? How could you do that to him?'

'He'll have other plans. I couldn't think of any other way to get rid of you...and it's worked, hasn't it?'

'What's worked?' Both girls spun round to see Strachan in the doorway, almost blocking out the narrow strip of light. 'Well?' he asked, when neither of them answered. His voice sounded dangerously calm and Gisella wondered if he thought that she was plotting again.

'She told Alan Wates about your plans for the centre,' Gisella said, when it was clear that the other girl was not about to admit to anything.

Elspeth clutched frantically at Strachan's arms. 'I didn't! You're not going to believe what she says, are you? She's the journalist! She's the one who came up here to poke and pry!'

Suddenly Gisella's precarious control over her misery shattered. 'No, he won't believe me!' she cried bitterly, and burst into tears. Horrified and ashamed at her weakness, she turned and stumbled blindly away across the rough lawn, heedless of the cold.

Strachan didn't try to stop her, and the tears poured down her cheeks as she realised that he was going to believe Elspeth after all, but the next instant there was a ripping sound as she found herself jerked to a halt. Bran had been sent bounding after her and had seized her skirt in his mouth.

'Let go!' Gisella begged, still crying, and tugged fruitlessly at the material. 'Drop, Bran!'

Bran merely sat down, keeping a tight hold on his captive, until Strachan reached them. At his master's command, he let her go obediently and sat looking pleased with himself, his tail wagging gently.

'He's torn my dress,' Gisella sobbed irrelevantly. It was the last straw.

Strachan took her firmly in his arms. She resisted, but he was too strong for her, and pulled her stiff body tightly against him. 'I'll buy you a new one,' he promised.

'You can't afford it,' she wept against his shoulder, too overwrought to think about what she was saying.

'I'll sell the castle,' he said. 'I'll do anything if you'll say you forgive me.' He rocked her against him as if she were a child. 'You don't really think I would believe Elspeth rather than you, do you?'

'You didn't believe me before.' Gisella's sobs had quietened to hiccuping snuffles, but she didn't try to pull away.

'I wasn't thinking straight,' Strachan said quietly. 'Try and imagine what I felt when I saw that article with your name in black and white. It was as if someone had kicked me in the stomach, thinking that you must have lied, that the last few days hadn't meant anything to you. I should have known you couldn't have done anything like that, in spite of how it seemed, but I was mad with shock and anger, and I couldn't see why your name should be on the story if you hadn't had anything to do with it.'

Her head was buried in his neck and he could feel the dampness of her tears against his collar as he stroked her hair. 'It was too easy to remember how bitter I'd felt against journalists since my father died, and to let myself think I'd been tricked and humiliated again.'

'I would never have done that to you,' Gisella said, her voice muffled.

He wrapped his arms more closely round her, feeling the distress slowly seeping out of her. 'I know, darling. I'll never forgive myself for the things I said to you. I was beside myself by then, but when you came down the stairs this evening you looked so beautiful that I forgot everything. I would have taken you in my arms there and then, but the Donalds got to you first and I remembered what a dedicated journalist you were.

'It was absolute hell being with you in front of all those people and not touching you. I knew that everything was wrong, and as soon as that wretched dance was over I was going to take you somewhere private and sort everything out. I didn't care if you *had* written the article, I just wanted you to stay. But then you disappeared suddenly, and I kept getting waylaid on my way to find you. Someone told me they'd seen you going outside, and I just got to the door in time to hear Elspeth saying that everything had worked out. As soon as you'd told me what she'd done, I knew it all made sense, but you ran off before I had a chance to tell you. I told Bran to catch you while I got rid of Elspeth, but I didn't mean him to tear the dress off you!'

'It doesn't matter.' The frost was seeping through Gisella's shoes and it was bitterly cold, but Gisella didn't care. With Strachan's arms warm about her and his heart beating reassuringly close, nothing mattered.

Strachan took Gisella's chin in his hand and tilted her face up to his. 'I'm afraid you're trapped, Gisella,' he said, but there was a smile in his voice as he saw the expression in her eyes. 'Bran isn't prepared to let you go, and neither am I. In fact, neither of us can contemplate life without you.'

'I'd better stay, then,' she said, and locked her arms about his neck as he gathered her close for a long, sweet kiss, where all was explained and all was forgiven without a word being said.

Afterwards, she rested her head against his shoulder and sighed with happiness and relief. 'It's just as well nobody believed us when we told them that we weren't engaged!'

'In that case, shall we go in and tell everyone what they already know?' suggested Strachan. 'What better time could there be to present the future lady of Kilnacroish? I want to make an announcement in front of everyone so that you can't change your mind!'

'I won't ever want to do that,' she promised with a kiss, and then looked down at herself with a grimace. 'Perhaps I should go and change first? You don't want a fiancée with a torn dress and a tear-stained face!'

'Yes, I do,' said Strachan. 'I want you just the way you are.'

Taking her hand, he whistled for Bran, and together they walked back across the frosty lawn towards the warmth and the light and the laughter.

Let

HARLEQUIN ROMANCE®

take you

BACK TO THE RANCH

Come to the Tully T Ranch near Fortune, Texas
(a blink-and-you'll-miss-it cow town!).

Meet Evelina Pettit, better known as Evvie, a schoolteacher from Houston who comes to help with the "Return to Good Fortune" celebrations. *And meet* rancher Ryan Garrison. He wants a wife—even though he doesn't believe in love. *Read* Virginia Hart's THE PERFECT SCOUNDREL and watch what happens when the schoolmarm meets the cowboy!

THE PERFECT SCOUNDREL is our next Back to the Ranch title, available in March,
wherever Harlequin Books are sold.

RANCH10

Relive the romance...
Harlequin and Silhouette
are proud to present

by Request™

A program of collections of three complete novels by the most-requested authors with the most-requested themes. Be sure to look for one volume each month with three complete novels by top-name authors.

In September: **BAD BOYS** — Dixie Browning, Ann Major, Ginna Gray

No heart is safe when these hot-blooded hunks are in town!

In October: **DREAMSCAPE** — Jayne Ann Krentz, Anne Stuart, Bobby Hutchinson

Something's happening! But is it love or magic?

In December: **SOLUTION: MARRIAGE** — Debbie Macomber, Annette Broadrick, Heather Graham Pozzessere

Marriages in name only have a way of leading to love....

Available at your favorite retail outlet.

REQ-G2

HARLEQUIN®   Silhouette

This Valentine's Day
give yourself something special. Something that's
just right for the most romantic day of the year.
Something that's all about love...

TWO FOR THE HEART

Two brand-new stories in one volume!
THE PROPOSAL by Betty Neels,
a favorite author for almost twenty-five years
and
THE ENGAGEMENT by Ellen James,
a new author with a fast-growing readership
Two brand-new stories that will satisfy,
charm and delight you!

HARLEQUIN ROMANCE®

From the heart and for the heart—
especially on Valentine's Day....
Available in February, wherever
Harlequin books are sold.

HRTFH

My Valentine 1994

Celebrate the most romantic day of the year with
MY VALENTINE 1994
a collection *of original stories, written by*
four of Harlequin's most popular authors...

MARGOT DALTON
MURIEL JENSEN
MARISA CARROLL
KAREN YOUNG

Available in February, wherever
Harlequin Books are sold.

HARLEQUIN®

VAL94

HARLEQUIN®

Don't miss these Harlequin favorites by some of our most distinguished authors!
And now, you can receive a discount by ordering two or more titles!

HT#25409	THE NIGHT IN SHINING ARMOR by JoAnn Ross	$2.99	☐
HT#25471	LOVESTORM by JoAnn Ross	$2.99	☐
HP#11463	THE WEDDING by Emma Darcy	$2.89	☐
HP#11592	THE LAST GRAND PASSION by Emma Darcy	$2.99	☐
HR#03188	DOUBLY DELICIOUS by Emma Goldrick	$2.89	☐
HR#03248	SAFE IN MY HEART by Leigh Michaels	$2.89	☐
HS#70464	CHILDREN OF THE HEART by Sally Garrett	$3.25	☐
HS#70524	STRING OF MIRACLES by Sally Garrett	$3.39	☐
HS#70500	THE SILENCE OF MIDNIGHT by Karen Young	$3.39	☐
HI#22178	SCHOOL FOR SPIES by Vickie York	$2.79	☐
HI#22212	DANGEROUS VINTAGE by Laura Pender	$2.89	☐
HI#22219	TORCH JOB by Patricia Rosemoor	$2.89	☐
HAR#16459	MACKENZIE'S BABY by Anne McAllister	$3.39	☐
HAR#16466	A COWBOY FOR CHRISTMAS by Anne McAllister	$3.39	☐
HAR#16462	THE PIRATE AND HIS LADY by Margaret St. George	$3.39	☐
HAR#16477	THE LAST REAL MAN by Rebecca Flanders	$3.39	☐
HH#28704	A CORNER OF HEAVEN by Theresa Michaels	$3.99	☐
HH#28707	LIGHT ON THE MOUNTAIN by Maura Seger	$3.99	☐

Harlequin Promotional Titles

#83247	YESTERDAY COMES TOMORROW by Rebecca Flanders	$4.99	☐
#83257	MY VALENTINE 1993 (short-story collection featuring Anne Stuart, Judith Arnold, Anne McAllister, Linda Randall Wisdom)	$4.99	☐

(limited quantities available on certain titles)

	AMOUNT	$
DEDUCT:	**10% DISCOUNT FOR 2+ BOOKS**	$
ADD:	**POSTAGE & HANDLING** ($1.00 for one book, 50¢ for each additional)	$
	APPLICABLE TAXES*	$ ________
	TOTAL PAYABLE (check or money order—please do not send cash)	$ ________

To order, complete this form and send it, along with a check or money order for the total above, payable to Harlequin Books, to: **In the U.S.:** 3010 Walden Avenue, P.O. Box 9047, Buffalo, NY 14269-9047; **In Canada:** P.O. Box 613, Fort Erie, Ontario, L2A 5X3.

Name: ______________________________

Address: ____________________ City: ____________

State/Prov.: ____________ Zip/Postal Code: ____________

*New York residents remit applicable sales taxes.
Canadian residents remit applicable GST and provincial taxes.

HBACK-JM